I've Got It Made

by

Jason A. Spencer-Edwards

JASP Publishing Inc.
Queens, New York

Published by JASP Publishing Inc.
133-16 230th Street, Queens, New York 11413
Email address: jasps@msn.com

Cover artwork by Garry T. Spoor
Book Cover Design: Garry T. Spoor and Jason A. Spencer-Edwards
Edited by: Betty Dobson, Lindsay Young, Jason A. Spencer-Edwards and
Kateline Gresseau

International Standard Book Number (ISBN): 978-1-4243-3131-4

Acknowledgements

First and foremost all thanks and praises go to God. I would also like to thank Kateline Gresseau, Fay, Cyril and Machael Edwards.

It was like clockwork. Every morning, Mr. Saks would get out of bed, and I could hear him moving towards the bathroom. I started counting backwards.

"Ten, nine, eight, seven, six, five, four, three, two, one."

I heard the all too familiar commotion, and, as Mr. Saks began speaking, I began moving my lips like a ventriloquist's dummy: *"I wish the superintendent would fix those broken tiles. I almost broke my neck!"*

Mr. Saks has been living above me and my family since I moved to this neighborhood five years ago. He was a grumpy old man who always seemed to be complaining about something or trying to "school" me and my crew. We often ignored him because he was old. He actually looked ancient. The running joke was that Mr. Saks is so old that he was given the first-ever social security number.

Math was never my best subject, but I knew by counting digits or place numbers that that was old because my social security number had nine digits.

Roger would chime in, "Nah. Mr. Saks is so old that he pees sand."

That's when Peter, who loved to add his two cents, jumped on the opportunity to tell a joke. "Mr. Saaaks is sooo, oooold thaaatt..."

"Peter, stop stuttering. By the time you get that joke out, we'll all be as old as Mr. Saks," Roger said.

Anytime Peter stuttered, I could tell something was wrong at home. His parents frequently had these intense fights after Peter's father would go out and drink at the local bar. In a drunken stupor, he used to trash the apartment, and the cops had to physically remove Peter's father from the apartment and have him cool off in jail for a night or so.

"Alcohol and drugs are so destructive," my mother would always say.

She was 100 percent right. They were lethal separately but a tsunami together. That is why my father didn't live with us anymore. He was addicted to both and spent all of our savings trying to satisfy his appetite.

Even though I was nine at the time, I remember it like it was yesterday when we were kicked out of our house in Selden, New York. I can see every square inch of our beautiful home without missing any detail.

As soon as you entered our house, you saw these huge columns. They reminded me of what I read about in history class when Mr. Green discussed the Greek Period and its architecture. Then you made your way to the kitchen, which included every appliance known to man.

This made cooking really easy, even though Mama never cooked; she had a maid for that.

Her name was Ms. Miles, and my father sent for her from London, England. Ms. Miles had the coolest English accent.

After dinner she would always say to my father, as he sat on the couch watching TV, "Would you like a cup of tea with some biscuits, Sir?"

Dad would laugh and repeat in his awful rendition of an English accent, "I would love a cup of tea and some biscuits. Cheerio."

Our living room was a sight to behold. It belonged in one of those house magazines under "decorating masterpieces." Or maybe in a museum where everyone could do what Ms. Miles liked to say: "Take a gander at this living room."

My mother had beautiful and expensive furniture neatly arranged in the room, and every detail was well thought out; everything in there complemented each other.

Ms. Miles religiously cleaned the living room once a day, seven days a week, from 9:30 to 11:30 in the morning. She entered the room wearing white gloves, wiping her fingers across the furniture, lamps, tables, picture frames—to locate any signs of dirt.

When she found any, she reacted like a doctor finding a strain of a deadly virus that was going to destroy the human race. "Oh dear. Oh dear. How did this get here? This has to go."

Me and my siblings were not allowed to go in that area for fear that we might dirty or ruin something. My mother would repeatedly say, "Don't go in there at all. I got that furniture from Italy, the rugs from India, lamps from France—and I don't want any sticky fingers or horseplay in there."

It was weird because my parents rarely went in there, and when they had guests, they just looked and commented, "How beautiful," and kept moving.

My parents had other rooms for different purposes. The greeting room was one; the entertainment room; cigar room; tea and coffee room; plus some other formal names as the adults sat, talked, and did other things.

The upstairs of our house reminded me of a hotel floor. We had about fifteen closed doors, many of which I never opened.

Our backyard was what Peter liked to call "hugemongous," topped off with a swimming pool with swim-up bar, remote control waterfall, two full-sized basketball courts, tennis court, Jacuzzi, and still enough land in the distance to build a mini-mall.

Those were the good old days.

Now we lived in an apartment building with twelve floors. Actually, I couldn't even tell you because the elevator was out most of the time; when the elevator did work you had to know what button to press because the numbers were scratched off.

The best word to describe our apartment was tiny. Ms. Miles' living quarters—actually, her dining room alone—was bigger than our whole apartment. Better yet, my parents' walk-in closet was bigger than our apartment.

Me, Marcus, and Alicia lived in the same room. Our room was so small that no furniture could fit inside. I was six feet five inches and slept on the top of the bunk bed. I thought that was a good idea five years ago, but since my growth spurt my legs would dangle off the bed. My brother Marcus was six feet three inches but had the bottom bunk. Lucky him! Alicia had a twin mattress, without a headboard or frame, placed up against the wall.

There was one window in my room that faced the back of the building. I never liked looking outside because it was depressing. Residents would throw garbage out their windows that would pile up outside.

Many nights I would be awakened by the loud thud the garbage made as it hit the rubble that had been sitting there for months.

I felt miserable for the moment but found my mother's words seeping into my head. "What doesn't kill you will make you stronger. Always look at the glass as being half full not half empty."

It always made me upset that my mother was so optimistic even though we had to live in this "*apartment building.*"

She would then say, "This place isn't so bad. It's just that some people are broken, baby. Don't you know that a bird with a broken wing can't fly? Not until its wings are mended can it take flight again. We just need a lot of mending and a lot of healing around here. I just keep on praying for changes."

I gave up on all that hocus-pocus five years ago when I prayed that my father wouldn't leave us and go away to Japan to work.

I jumped out of bed as soon as I heard Mr. Saks flush the toilet bowl. Jumping up and down off the top bunk was like Mr. Saks: getting old.

My apartment building's plumbing was terrible. It should have been named *Leaky Projects*. Everyone in my building had at least one horror story on how the plumbing has affected them in some manner: ruined carpets and furniture, and sometimes completely flooded apartments.

I was sick and tired of getting sprinkled with drops of water every time he flushed the toilet. Man! I wished he could put a cork in it.

* * *

At last month's building meeting, Mr. Billings had Mr. Brown—the building's superintendent, who was as useful as a flat tire on a rainy night—give updates on the building. Mr. Billings' name fit him to a tee—because if you were one day late on your rent, he was ready to evict you faster than a speeding bullet—and he also never showed up to any meeting unless it was to collect outstanding rent. His favorite line was, "Bills have to be paid."

Mr. Brown was an overweight, short-tempered man who looked like he cut his hair himself. It was never even, and the sides of his hair were gray and the top and back were colored jet black.

He waddled up to the microphone carrying his favorite food, brownies, in his left hand. He practically inhaled a brownie before he spoke.

With crumbs all over his mouth and shirt he said, "Tenants, I have been extremely busy. I have been doing other repairs, and rest assured that plumbing is a high priority. It will be the next thing I do. I promise. Thank you and have a good night."

Mr. Brown must be really busy because he has been telling that story to my mother for about five years.

* * *

I opened the door and headed to the bathroom. I turned on the light and saw a huge roach relaxing on the floor next to the toilet bowl. *I hated roaches. They are ugly and disgusting. I heard that if we had a nuclear war they would be one of the few things that would survive.*

This was a bad sign. He didn't even move as I approached. If I saw one, that meant there were more around; before you knew it, they'd be having a nightly convention.

I hurried outside the bathroom and grabbed a shoe that was sitting by the door and hit the roach as hard as I could.

"Humankind one point. Roaches zero," I said, when I noticed that the roach had stopped moving.

I tore a piece of toilet paper from the roll on the wall and scooped up the roach carefully and wrapped it up nice and neat to give it a proper burial and opened the toilet bowl.

I was startled when I felt a twitching sensation through the toilet paper.

I looked back at the toilet paper and that *NASTY, DISGUSTING, UGLY ROACH* came out the other side and was crawling up my arm. I didn't want to squash it on me for fear of getting the *cooties.*

This was bad; if I got the cooties, then I would need the *"cooties shot,"* and we didn't have any health insurance. I began vigorously shaking the whole right side of my body, and the roach dropped off my arm. Before it hit the ground, it spread its wings and began flying around me like a vulture.

I was terrified. "Ah, Ah, Ahhhh, Ahhhhhhh!"

I headed for the bathroom door without even looking back.

As soon as I got outside, I saw my mother standing there with her hands on her hips. "Boy, are you trying to wake up the whole building? Why are you screaming? Have you lost your mind?"

It felt like my heart was going to jump out of my chest. I had to catch my breath before I spoke.

"Sorry, Mama, but I just saw a flying roach."

She started laughing. "Boy, you must be seeing things. They don't have those things in this country."

"Mama, I'm telling you I just saw one."

My mother wasn't afraid of insects or anything that moved. She went inside and came back out and said, "Whatever you say you saw isn't in there anymore."

"Thanks, Mama," I said as my heartbeat returned to normal.

I went back in the bathroom and looked around nervously as I urinated. I finished up quickly, and I went to our kitchen and watched as Mama put the kettle on the stove.

My mother had to take out a match and light the lighter because it always went right out after you used it, so we had plenty of matches on hand.

I stared deep into my mother's eyes and saw how tired she looked. She was actually gearing up to leave for her first shift. She had two jobs: one was working as a checkout clerk at a twenty-four-hour convenience store, which she worked from 5 a.m. to 11 a.m.; from 12 p.m. to 8 p.m., she worked as a waitress downtown at this fancy five star restaurant.

"How you doing, baby? Why are you up so early? It's four in the morning."

"Mr. Saks was talking, peeing, and next came the dripping of water."

"Baby, I am so sorry. I have to talk to Mr. Brown again."

"Mama, you've been talking to him for about five years. This place is a dump. Why do we have to live here?"

"Honey, we've been through this before. This won't be permanent. Trust me. I'm searching for an answer. Be patient."

"Mama, we don't need a search party. We need money. Money will solve all our problems," I replied. "If we had enough then our life would be a hundred times better."

"Look sugar. Money doesn't answer all your questions or solve all your problems. Look around; there are more important things than just that."

"Are you kidding? Like what?"

My mother was in no mood to continue the conversation and crossed her arms and twitched her right eyebrow, which meant I was barking up the wrong tree.

"Look, sugar, I'm going to work. I'll see you later," she said, gulping down the last of her coffee. "Make sure your brothers and sister are fine. Now come over here and give me a big hug."

My mother came up to my chest, standing at a whopping five feet five inches. She looked up and said, "Boy, you better stop growing, or I'll need a ladder to get to you. Bend down here and give your mother a kiss."

I slouched down and kissed her on the cheek and helped her put her coat on as she left the apartment.

It was about 4:45 a.m., and I knew that I couldn't go back to sleep. I went into our living room and sat on our white couch, which really needed to be thrown away. It had so many black stains on it that it looked like a Dalmatian.

I found the remote under the couch and turned on the TV. I listened as a real estate guru was talking about the good life: *fast cars, big homes, clothes, costly vacations, jewelry, and money to burn.*

To prove that money wasn't a thing, he began fanning himself with the money that lay out on a table as he sat by the pool with some models surrounding him like the Secret Service protecting the President.

I turned the station quickly because it made me sick to my stomach. My family had that and more, and now, five years later, we were stuck in this tiny apartment.

I kept channel surfing and jumped to the cartoon channel. I loved cartoons and needed to cheer myself up and laughed uncontrollably when a furry little creature farted out loud.

My youngest brother, Albert—who was five years old going on twenty-five—came out of my mother's room. He spotted me on the couch and took a running leap and landed in my arms. "Cowabunga, dude."

"You've been watching too much *Teenage Mutant Ninja Turtles*," I said, tickling him.

"I'm hungry. Can I have some cereal?"

"Okay. I'll get it during the next commercial."

"Okay," he said as he focused on the cartoon.

I continued watching and laughing, and soon Alicia was up.

"What's all that noise? I am going to tell Mama when she comes home. Don't you know a woman needs her sleep?"

"Newsflash. You are in the third grade. Woman? Ppplease. How old are you again?"

"A woman never tells her age. So don't bother asking!"

I began laughing. "Okay, Miss Thing. Get Albert some cereal."

She put her hands on her hips and answered, "That is not my responsibility. If you want me to help you, it will cost you twenty dollars."

I snickered. "Why would I pay you even a penny? Little girl, go somewhere."

"I'll tell you why. Because if you don't, I'll tell Mama you had some of your friends over here last week. You know, on a school night. So, Mister Smartie Pants, it could be twenty dollars or maybe twenty days of punishment or, even worse, some hand-to-hand combat with Mama. You know, kind of like those dumb video games you and your friends like playing. But for you, the rules will be slightly different. You'll be the one receiving the beating. And boy will it be real."

I was heated. If Mama knew I had some of the crew over on a school night, she would have my behind. I could hear her saying, *"I brought you into this world, and I can take you out."*

"Take it out of my piggy bank."

I hated taking money out of my piggy bank. I was saving every penny I got to get this new game system called the VGA2 that came out last week. That hit me hard because with that withdrawal I only had forty-five dollars left. At this pace, I would get the VGA2 that cost $700 when I was a senior citizen.

My sister pranced in front of me. "Money, money, money, money, monniee, monnieee."

I wanted to hurl when she sang. Alicia was like a sponge; she talked and acted like a grown-up even though she was only eight years old. She was far from the average third grader, and she enjoyed showing off the new words she could pronounce and use in a sentence.

"It was nice doing business with you," she said as she sat next to me on the couch.

Marcus came into the living room next, and I had officially awakened the whole gang.

"Have you seen my math book? I need to get some practice in."

Marcus was a straight "A" student, and his pastime was books. He started reading at four years old and used to read bedtime stories to my parents. He read all kinds of books, and every week my mother would buy him a new book, which, when he was finished, he tried to pass down to me.

I once saw her credit card bills. She was making minimum payments (twenty dollars a month) on a $10,000 balance from purchasing textbooks, novels, and other reading and writing materials in different subjects.

To me, this kind of behavior was pathetic.

If my mother would take some of that money along with all that other money she used for museum trips and DVDs that she purchased for Alicia and Albert, we could have somewhat of a down payment on another home.

Mama's favorite line was, "The best investment one can make is on one's education. It will reap benefits for as long as you live. Once you have that knowledge in your head, no one can take that away from you. No one."

When she jumped on her soapbox, I would appear interested, but I didn't care too much for school.

"Why go to school? You go to school to make money, right? Well, if I start making money now, I'll have a head start on everyone else that is spending years and years in school." That's how Fred would have responded to my mother.

Fred was one of my closest homies and was the first person I met when I moved to this neighborhood. Fred was eighteen years old and dropped out of school when he was my age, fourteen. He had been doing odd jobs here and there, and I never quite knew where he lived. He seemed to pop up out of nowhere, and I never understood where he got the money to look so fly every day. He had shown me the do's and the don'ts in our neighborhood, and that helped me out of many possibly life-threatening situations.

Fred would tell me, "Forget book smarts. I have street smarts, and that's all I need. Once you have that, you can eat off these streets forever."

I never asked him too many questions, because that was one of his most important rules. "*Keep your eyes on your fries.*"

"What the heck does that mean?"

"That is symbolism, young'un. The fries represent your life, and if you are focusing on someone else's stuff you might lose your own."

Fred knew I was lost in the sauce and added, "Mind your business, and you get to live longer."

I jumped up and told Marcus that his math book was under the couch.

I had to get dressed for school and put on the iron and went back to a small closet that held me and my siblings' clothes. I grabbed some white corduroy pants and my gray sweatshirt. I found my gray sneakers and looked at the scuffmark that went across the front of my sneaker. That happened yesterday as this little boy ran over my foot with his tricycle while I was walking through the park. He didn't even say sorry. I should have given him a wedgie.

With the rag I found in the bathroom, I got some bleach and mixed it with some Ajax and began scrubbing. That concoction was lethal, and Alicia came to the bathroom door.

"What is that smell?"

"Don't worry about it."

"You better watch your tone, or maybe I'll see what Mama thinks."

I stopped scrubbing because I was getting dizzy and it wasn't worth it; those sneakers needed to be thrown away.

I ran the iron over my pants and realized after ten minutes that they were still wrinkled. I pressed the steam button, and the iron made a loud hissing sound then I saw a cloud of steam rushing out of the iron. When the smoke cleared, I looked down on my pants and saw rusty, brown spots. "This stupid iron. We need another one. It just ruined my pants."

Marcus came over to see what all the fuss was about. "I read somewhere that if you mix baking soda with liquid soap on the stain, it will come right out."

I ignored him initially but decided to give it a shot because nothing else I tried was working. The stains miraculously came out, and my brother had a grin on his face that went from ear to ear.

"Knowledge is power, big brother, and if you read more, you'll have enough knowledge to last you five lifetimes."

"Look, bro, good looking for the suggestion and everything but don't get it twisted. I don't want you to try to recruit me into your group of misfits. What is it you call yourself again?"

Before he answered I quickly responded, "Oh yeah, I remember. You call yourself the RAUFAM Club."

Marcus shook his head in disgust and said, "No, that is RAUTAM: short for Reading Allows You To Achieve More."

"Achieve what again?" I said, trying not to crack up.

"Achieve anything you put your mind to. Knowledge is power."

I was sick of his little soliloquies. "Well, Mr. RAUTAM, one day you'll be joining my crew."

"What's that?"

"MIP."

"What does that stand for?"

"*MONEY IS POWER.* Once you have money, you don't need anything else."

My brother turned around and didn't respond; he went back to the table and buried his head in his math textbook.

I made sure Alicia and Albert were clean and dressed, and we all headed for the door. As soon as I got outside my building, I saw Peter waiting patiently with his hands in his pockets.

"What's up, everyone?"

"Nothing. Chilling. What's good?"

Peter had dark circles around his eyes like he hadn't slept at all, and I didn't need to be clairvoyant to know that it had something to do with his parents fighting again.

We began our six-block trek to school. It was kind of weird not having Roger around; he had to move down south last week to be close to his grandmother, who had breast cancer and was going through chemotherapy.

It was cold outside, and the wind appeared to have a vendetta against us. Snow was already on the ground, and I wished it was summertime. I didn't talk much because I could hardly feel my hands.

It felt minus twenty degrees out there.

Our neighborhood was a mess. Most of the time, it looked like a junkyard: old mattresses piled up outside in vacant lots, empty beer and liquor bottles, food containers from the local Chinese food restaurant, potato chip bags, soda and juice bottles, scattered newspapers, and flyers. Some people didn't believe in placing anything in the garbage.

I stepped on an empty milk carton, and Alicia started laughing.

"Milk does a body good," she said while putting her hands in her pockets.

We continued walking, and I saw a group of men standing around a huge iron-like container with fire coming out of it trying to keep their hands warm. They were going on about last night's basketball game and how the Knicks blew it again.

Through my peripheral view, I saw a homeless-looking man approaching the group. His lips were white and crusty, and he looked like he hadn't bathed or combed his hair in months. They saw him try to get even closer and screamed, "Get lost, you bum, and wash up. You smell like elephant dung."

"Your Momma," the homeless-looking man answered. "That is not what she told me when she took me out to dinner last night."

They began chasing him, but he was fast.

As the distance widened after each step they took, they wisely abandoned chase. The homeless-looking man, who was a full block away, shouted, "You guys are slower than molasses. I was a star runner in college. I could run laps around you clowns."

The fattest one out of the group, who had his hands on his knees trying to catch his breath, shouted back, "So you are training for the Olympics, huh? Well, I guess you found something you like better than running. Like drugs, you crackhead. Go wash, you smelly vagabond."

The homeless man danced around, taunting them to come get him; when they ignored him, he disappeared around the corner, and we continued walking.

Alicia began reciting, "Dung, the definition: the excrement of animals."

I turned to her and said, "The *what* of animals?"

"The excrement of animals," she said with her index finger on her chin. "Excuse me. I am so sorry. I will speak English for you. Excrement means waste matter discharged from the body."

"What are you talking about?"

She put her hands on her hips. "I give up. Feces. Get it. Feces. Or do I have to tell you what that means, too? You need to read more. You're such a dumpkoff."

Peter and Marcus burst into laughter, and I wanted to slap the taste out of my sister's mouth. I hated being embarrassed. I didn't know what that meant either, and I wasn't going to ask any more questions before I really lost my cool and did something that I would later regret.

Peter saw I was baffled; as we walked, he whispered, "That means a stupid person, a dumbbell, a blockhead. You didn't do last week's homework, did you?"

I shook my head. I felt homework was for chumps. *Educate me with a large bank account. If you give me money, I'll show you how to "ball out of control,"* I thought.

We finally reached the school entrance and went up to the security guard. Last year someone brought a weapon to school, so now everyone had to go through metal detectors. I guess safety was the number one priority, even though it felt like I was in jail and hated taking off my belt, watch and sneakers and anything else that was considered a place to hide something.

We were used to the routine and always complied with their wishes. As the security guard put our bags through the scanner, she motioned for us to go through one at a time. Albert went through first; when the security guard waved her wand over his body, he began shaking like he was having a seizure.

Peter looked worried and began panicking.

"What's wrong with him? Is he having a seizure right now?"

Albert suddenly dropped to the ground and began shaking even more.

I turned to the security guard.

"Call the ambulance."

The security guard looked like she had seen a ghost and began panicking. "What is the number for the ambulance?"

That sounded funny to me, and I began laughing. "I am not sure. Is it 119 or 911?"

Alicia joined in and began laughing while Peter stood frozen.

The security guard yelled, "What is so funny? Don't you see that your brother is sick?"

I became serious and said, "Okay, okay. Help me pin him down."

I began holding his feet, and I told Alicia to hold down his shoulders.

"We need to put something in his mouth so he doesn't swallow his tongue."

I gave the security guard my leather belt and she began moving closer to my brother's face. She was in breathing distance, almost face to face, when Albert broke free of her arms and kissed her right on the lips.

The security guard was shocked, and Albert began giggling.

She was upset and said, "Why you sneaky little..."

"I'm sorry. I'm so sorry," he said with his big, light brown eyes smiling up at her. "You are so pretty. I couldn't help myself. Are you a model? Will you marry me?"

She shook her head, smiled, and said, "Find your way to class before I march you all off to the Principal's Office."

I went to the basement and dropped off Albert at his first grade class. Alicia knew her way and went to the first floor. Peter went to the third floor.

One positive thing about our school was that they had Pre-K-8 in the same building. I was in the eighth grade, and Marcus who was eleven was in the seventh grade, even though he really belonged in the fifth grade.

At the rate he was skipping grades, he would be finished with high school right before he turned sixteen.

This was a constant reminder as I walked around school. Marcus was the poster boy for academic excellence and achievement, and most teachers would ask if we were related.

Mr. Jones, my math teacher, joked last week and said, "Are you sure that you are related? Maybe the stork dropped off the wrong bundle, and you were supposed to be dropped off at the zoo." That joke received a long laugh from my classmates. When anyone dissed me, I usually had a quick comeback, but since I was already on the path of failing for the second semester, I decided to ignore him. I vowed to get him back some day.

I went to homeroom class, but I really wanted to be back home sleeping. Instead, I began thinking how was I going to get the money—a.k.a. guap, scrilla, Benjamins, cheddar, cheese, dead presidents, greenbacks—for the remaining $655 for the VGA2.

I drew a huge blank because I wasn't about to work at a minimum wage paying job.

I looked towards the front of the class and saw Roxanne Fletcher. The hottest girl (cayenne pepper hot) in the school, and somebody who I have had my eyes on since I was in the sixth grade. My nickname for her, which I never blurted out, was "Foxy Roxy."

She was beyond beautiful. Perfect shape, perfect height, perfect teeth, perfect smile, perfect hair—the list goes on and on. Please! She put the P in perfection.

Once Brandon (the boy who was so creepy that even the weirdest kids in school avoided him) tried asking Roxanne out on a date. Roxanne scrunched up her face and rudely responded, "Look, Brandon. Take a real good look at me. I am a Lamborghini, and you are a Hooptie. I am all the fly and expensive stuff you see in the stores, and you are the flea market hand-me-downs. When you step your game up, I mean potential wise and all that, maybe I will part my lips to say hello. If would also help if you were cool, popular or a jock. You are presently polluting my environment. Please don't enter my airspace again."

After that fiasco, I never approached her because I was none of those things and dared not "play myself."

It was time to enter the world of "Make Believe."

I closed my eyes and wished with all my might that I was Roxanne's man. I decided to really envision it, and I put my head on the desk to make myself more comfortable.

Ten minutes later, I was jolted out of my sleep by the sound of the bell ringing. I was mad. I was just about to get a kiss from Roxanne.

As I picked up my head, I saw Roxanne walking towards me. When she got right in front of my desk, I could hardly keep my smile in and she said my name. "Justin."

"Yes," I answered, as this was the first time she had spoken to me.

It seemed so natural, I wanted her to say it over and over again. I tried to look sexy and licked my lips as she said it again.

"Justin."

"Yes, Roxanne."

I had officially called her name out loud. This was heaven sent!

Roxanne's lips began moving again. "You have globs of spit on your sleeve. That is nasty!"

I was so embarrassed and wanted to fix the problem right away. I tried wiping off the spit on my sleeve, and it came flying off me and landed on Roxanne's white skirt.

I tried cleaning it off with my hand and made it even dirtier.

She was fuming. "Look what you have done. Stay away from me, you imbecile."

That was another word that didn't ring a bell, and I bet Alicia knew the meaning. One thing I did know was that I was being insulted.

Roxanne quickly walked away from me, and her friends looked at me and just shook their heads.

"See, girls? See what happens when you talk to people on the lower end of the totem pole? Bad things happen."

I left homeroom feeling stupid and went straight to math class. Oh joy! I had Mr. Jones.

He assigned me a seat right in front of his desk at the beginning of the semester, and I think he enjoyed making me the butt of his jokes.

The late bell rang, and he started writing the objective on the board.

"Attention, class. Before you get started on the examples on the board, can everyone pass your homework assignment up to the front of the classroom? Need I remind you that homework counts for twenty-five percent of your grade?"

I didn't bother going into my bookbag because I didn't do it. What was the point of learning all these mathematical formulas? I could add and subtract, and that's all I needed to know.

"Well, well, Justin. No homework again. What's the excuse this time? Dog ate your homework? Oh no, that was last week. Maybe the cat peed on it. Oh, that was yesterday. Justin, let's be honest; you don't care at all. Oh, maybe the elevator in your head is not going to the top floor."

Everyone started laughing, and I was sick and tired of Mr. Jones' insults. "That is real funny. One day I'll be mega-rich, and then you'll see. I am going to make sure that when I do 'blow up' you see me in my car, clothes—'looking fresh to death.' Then I'll have the last laugh."

Mr. Jones put his hand on his cheeks and slowly waved his head back and forth and sighed. "I don't know about that. But the probability of that happening is more than likely...not going to happen. What makes you think you are so special?"

"*What makes you an authority on me? This school thing is getting tired. I'm out of here.*"

I jumped out of my seat and left the classroom and slammed the door as I exited. I headed down the hallway and went to the basement, avoiding the security guards that patrolled the school. I went through the janitor's exit downstairs that didn't have an alarm and made my way to the train station.

Like Harry Houdini, Fred seemed to appear out of thin air.

"What's up, Justin? Yo, where you going?"

"I don't know. Away from school. That place makes me want to vomit," I answered, trying to get as far away from school as quickly as possible.

"I hear that. Slow your roll."

I slowed down so Fred could catch up to me.

"You know they'll be calling your house tonight."

"Let them call. I don't care. I'm sick of all these rules and regulations and what I should do and how school is important. I'm really tired of being beaten in the head with all this mumbo-jumbo."

Fred smiled. "I feel you completely. That's why school was history for me at your age, and four years later I'm still looking fly and getting money. Doing it like I am doing it for TV. That's my American Dream."

I looked at Fred and noticed he had the tags still attached to his jacket, pants, and shirt. When he noticed I was staring, he pushed them back in. I wanted to ask him where he got it, but I remembered, *"Keep your eyes on your fries."*

The wind started blowing as we continued walking up the street and I wished I had on the black snorkel jacket that was covering his head.

Fred said, "Yo, check it. Since we are both outside, let's go to the city, maybe Times Square, and walk around."

I went in my pockets, pulled them inside out, and said, "I have nothing in my pockets except lint balls."

Fred burst into laughter.

"Don't worry about that. I got you. I got paid yesterday. Actually, every day for me is payday. Tax free. No state, federal, local, social security, or some other people that shouldn't be seeing no parts of my money. Uncle Sam isn't kin to me."

Fred went inside his pocket and pulled out a wad of hundreds and started counting it aloud.

"This is all the school I need. One, two, buckle my shoe; three, four, I get money galore; five, six, buying a platinum and gold crucifix; seven, eight, my sneaker game is straight; nine, ten, tomorrow I'll be getting money again." Fred snickered. "Do you like my nursery rhyme? I could have been a rapper. But nah, most of those rappers don't have money anyway. Most of them just fronting."

Fred continued rhyming, but he got bored when he got to twenty-five. I wished I had all that money, but I was happy that I wasn't hanging out alone.

I watched some truant officers coming around the block and we quickly ran down the stairs into the train station. I didn't need to get busted and sent back to school.

Fred paid for my Metro-card, and we got on the train that just pulled in. Everyone reminded me of conditioned rats, running around bumping into one another until they found a seat, then appearing relieved as they would fall asleep as the train moved along.

Every train stop was the same exact scenario. It was hilarious seeing adults doing the same thing over and over again. Is that what I had to look forward to? No way was I going out like that. Just worrying about working and surviving. How boring.

There was a foul smell on the train; when I looked in the corner, I saw a homeless man. Fred was disgusted and whispered in my ear, "I am never going to be like that. Obviously he didn't graduate from my school of Getting Money University. I should teach a course in it."

I put myself out a limb, expecting to be snatched back like a rubber band. "How do you get money?"

His answer rolled off his tongue effortlessly. "By any means necessary. When I think you are ready, I'll show you a thing or two."

I didn't quite know what that meant, but anything that required no school would be an excellent idea.

Forty-five minutes later, we got off the train. The city was so attractive; they had these great big billboards and everyone seemed to be moving quickly. A tourist bumped into Fred and stepped on his sneaker, and I had to restrain him from smacking the old lady.

"Can you believe her? I can't wear these sneakers anymore; they are ruined."

I looked at the barely visible scratch mark on the front of his sneaker and had to keep from saying, "You are really bugging."

"I always have to be fresh to death. You hear me? Fresh to death," Fred said, looking at the lady, who just stood there paralyzed. "Let's go in this sneaker store."

We went inside a Foot Locker, and Fred began looking around.

A sales clerk approached as Fred began picking up a sneaker.

"Can I help you?" the store clerk asked as Fred moved on to another sneaker.

Fred responded, "Do you have the newer version of the sneaker that I have on my feet in size ten and a half?"

"I'll have to check in the back."

I sat down, trying not to look at anything because I had the same pair of sneakers for about eight months and no money for an upgrade.

The sales clerk came back with Fred's sneakers; as Fred tried them on, the sales clerk asked, "How do they feel?"

"They are okay," Fred answered, not really paying attention to him as he laced them up.

When I looked at the empty box, I saw they were $175.

Fred paced up and down in the store, testing the sneakers for comfort.

"These are cool. Do you have them in other colors?"

"We sure do. We have them in blue, red, and white."

"Alright, that's cool. Bring them out. I'll take them."

"Excuse me. You do know, they are $175 a piece," the sales clerk said as he pointed to the price on the box.

Fred got loud and animated. "What's your point? Did I tell you I didn't have the money? Do your job. You are a minimum wage worker, which means you don't get paid enough money to ask dumb questions. Do I look like a bum or something?"

The sales clerk had his mouth open and Fred proved his point by going into his pocket, taking out two hundred-dollar bills and ripping them into little pieces.

"Money ain't a thing. Do me a favor, Mr. Minimum Wage. Get all the sneakers I requested and take them up to the counter."

The clerk was disgusted, and Fred made sure to speak to the manager of the store about customer care. Shortly afterwards, I looked over and saw the manager chewing the sales clerk out while he had his head down in shame.

Fred put on the first pair of sneakers he tried on and left the box on the counter. Then he put the sneakers he came into the store with on the counter and told the clerk, "Be a sport and discard everything for me."

We left the store and continued walking up 34th Street. I was blinded by the huge billboard displaying the VGA2 gaming system.

I turned to Fred. "Yo, check it. That is the game system I wanted to get, but my funds are hurting. It just came out last week, and they only shipped 300 of them to New York."

"I didn't know you are into video games." Fred said, as he gave another tourist a dirty look as he almost stepped on his sneakers.

"I love video games. My father bought me my first gaming system when I was eight."

"That's kid stuff. Fantasy world things. Make believe."

"Nah. That stuff is hot. You must be loony."

"If you say so."

We kept walking and went into this burger joint, and Fred ordered a extra large vanilla milkshake, French fries, onion rings, and a bacon double cheeseburger with the works. Fred was feeling generous, and I ordered the same.

Our meal was interrupted when a stranger approached our table. "What's up, Fred?"

Fred looked at him and said, "Do I know you?"

"You forgot already. It's me."

Fred looked closer at the guy and said, "Yo! My fault. What's up, George? Where have you been these days?"

"Just working in the electronics store across the street. When you are done, come check me. I'm on my lunch break."

"That's cool. I'll holla in a minute."

Curiosity had gotten the best of me, and I inquired about George. "Who was that?"

"Some geek I went to high school with. He was a senior when I was a freshman. Word is he graduated from college and everything but couldn't find a job. Now he is working across the street for minimum wage. Can you believe he was voted most likely to succeed in his graduating class yearbook?"

Fred slurped on his milkshake, "I'm glad that I dropped out. That could have been me, too, working for minimum wage and all."

I sat back and continued eating because that bacon double cheeseburger was heavenly. When we were finished we made our way across to the electronics store, and I saw the VGA2 again.

"I'm telling you, Fred, that system is fire. Look at the graphics; it is incredible. Tell me that doesn't look real."

Fred looked disinterested and started fiddling with some camcorders that were on display.

George spotted me and came over to me. "That system is off the hook, right."

"Tell me about it. All those features, and the graphics are unreal."

George came close to me and whispered so no one else in the store could make out what he was saying. "We just got a shipment in today, and I am supposed to put a sign outside telling the public we have it. It is going to be a stampede in here."

Fred came over to us and said, "What are you two whispering about?"

"The VGA2. That system is bananas," I said in an animated voice.

"It's alright. You still talking about this thing?" Fred answered while looking at a girl that walked past us.

"Are you kidding me? I would die for one," I replied.

Fred turned his attention to George. "How much for that?"

"It is $700 and you have to get this game that just came with it. They only have 200 copies of this game in circulation around the world, and only twenty have been shipped to New York."

"Okay. Okay. Stop all this video game talk. What's the total?"

George took out a calculator from his pocket and started punching numbers. "With all these accessories, extra controller, memory card, power pack, carrying case..."

Fred was getting impatient. "I don't have all day. Time is money."

George pushed his glasses up on his nose and said, "It will be $1,001.28."

I closed my eyes and drew in a deep breath.

"It's nothing to a boss," Fred said, as he went in his pocket and counted out eleven hundred-dollar bills.

"George, keep the change."

"Thanks man. I really appreciate that," I said as I gave Fred a bear hug.

Fred gave a look that said, "Pause." That's when I remembered another one of his rules for survival: "Showing emotion can get your life span shortened."

I didn't care. I started dancing around like a eight-year-old that had had too much caffeine.

Fred still had the pause look on his face, so I began dancing faster and faster until Fred started cracking up. I had the whole store cheering me on, and people started chanting, "Go head, go head, go head, go head."

I finished up my dance routine by doing my Michael Jackson rendition and pulled up my shirt and screamed, "OOOOOOHHHH! ooooohh, ooooh. Hee-Heee-Heeee."

It was almost 1:15, and I knew I had to hurry up to get back to school. If I didn't make it, my siblings knew to wait fifteen minutes after the last bell rang; then they should all walk home together.

We quickly made our way to the train station. I used my Metro-card and went through the turnstile; I looked back at Fred and saw him jumping the turnstile.

As he made his way down the platform, I asked, "Why did you do that? You have the money and a Metro-card, too."

Fred crossed his arms and said, "Chill out. What is life without excitement? Plus there is never any cops around here, and if they were around they would have arrested me already."

We waited for the train, and the platform was packed. I made sure that I wasn't too close to the edge of the platform because I heard about people getting pushed down onto the tracks.

A middle-aged man with long gray hair and a bushy moustache slowly approached us. I could tell there was something odd about him. He began eyeballing Fred; before I could figure out why, Fred started running. "Yo, later Justin. It's Popo."

I was confused. The man didn't have a policeman's uniform on.

As I turned my back to the wall, trying to look inconspicuous, he ran past me speaking in number codes on his walkie-talkie while still giving chase. "We got a runner. I need backup. Over and out."

Fred was fast, and I was amazed how quickly he moved without a belt in his pants. Fred had the sneaker bags in both arms and was dodging straphangers like he was going through an obstacle course.

"Stop. Police. Young man, stop." The officer yelled who had no chance of catching up to Fred.

A train began pulling into the station; since they didn't stop me, I got on an empty car and had a seat.

After sitting there for about fifteen minutes, the conductor announced that the train had been ordered to remain in the station. I peeked outside the open doors and saw Fred's face pinned against the platform floor with his sneaker boxes scattered all around him.

One officer who was in uniform asked, "Where do you think you were going? We know you jumped that turnstile; the subway camera caught you."

They began searching through his pockets, and an officer who looked like he only ran to the donut counter said, "Look what we have here. Where did you get this money from? Are you a thief or a drug dealer?"

Fred turned to him and calmly answered, "Nah. I'm neither. Ask your wife. We are real good friends. We have a great understanding. She gives me half of your paycheck every week."

The officer wasn't pleased with Fred's smart mouth; as he began putting on the handcuffs, he made sure they were extra tight. I heard Fred howl in pain.

The officer signaled to the conductor to move the train, and I fell asleep during my ride back to Queens.

I was in front of my school right before the bell rang, and was relieved to be back in my neighborhood. Marcus was exiting the school with Albert, and Alicia and Peter were close behind.

As soon as Alicia saw the bag in my hand, she started shooting off at the mouth. "What's inside the bag?"

"None of your business. I am holding it for a friend."

"A friend, huh? I hope it isn't that loser Fred who you like to look up to."

"Shut up, Alicia. I've had enough of your mouth."

"If you even breathe on me hard, I'm telling Mama."

I gave the bag to Peter and told him I would pick it up later that evening.

The elevator was out again, and I had to walk up ten flights.

I came in the apartment out of breath, went in the refrigerator and took out the cherry Kool-Aid, and began gulping some down. It was like everyone had the same idea, and with my siblings going back for seconds, the pitcher was sitting in the sink empty.

Marcus sat down on the floor a couple of steps from the bathroom, took out his math book, and began working on a math problem, talking out loud, trying to figure out how he was going to attack the problem. Albert was near Mama's room, playing with his Teenage Mutant Ninja Turtle toys, and Alicia was reading the dictionary.

I needed to get some sleep. I was exhausted. I went to my room, but I had a hard time falling asleep because I kept thinking about Fred and what happened to him earlier on.

I don't know how long I was out because I was abruptly awakened by a crashing sound. When I ran into the living room, Albert had broken a glass and was sitting on the broken pieces.

I shouted at Marcus, who still had his head buried in his math book.

"You should be watching him. Mama is going to have a fit."

Alicia butted in. "You're the oldest, so you are going to be the one in trouble."

I ignored her and went to the couch and turned on the TV, as Marcus cleaned up the broken glass. I hated the fact that our TV was so small. I would have loved if we had one of those fifty-inch plasma flat screen TVs.

I was hypnotized as I saw a commercial about the VGA2. *"The system of all systems. If you get one, you don't need anything else."*

Marcus and Alicia heard the commercial playing and got up and sat on the couch next to me, staring at the TV.

Alicia said, "Those graphics are stupendous. I wish we had one."

I turned to them and said, "I could get one if I wanted."
Marcus chuckled. "Yeah, right, big brother. They are all sold out. Plus they run about $800."

I wanted to share my secret, but if they found out that I had one and told Mama, she would have my head for accepting gifts from people. She would say, "We don't need handouts; we have all the basic necessities."

Mama was so hypocritical. Now all of a sudden she was singing, "Kumbaya, my lord, Kumbaya. Oh Lord, Kumbaya."

When we were rich, she used to go shopping every other day. Mama had a Black Card and was definitely fresh to death. Now she just wants the basics. I want the lifestyle we used to have.

I decided to go to Peter's apartment and play my VGA2.

I had to pay Alicia $10 to watch Albert because Marcus was on his way to the library to get more books.

Marcus and I walked out of the apartment; when we reached the bottom of the stairs, we went our separate ways.

I went across to Peter's building; fortunately for me, his elevator was working. Entering his apartment was an unforgettable experience. The apartment was immaculate [Alicia used that word to describe her side of our room].

Peter's mother had a flair for interior design. She seemed way too talented to be a Parks Department worker. Cleaning up garbage and stuff like that.

Peter told me that she had gotten accepted into an Art and Design School on full college scholarship, but she had gotten pregnant with him before she started school and couldn't go. Peter's parents got married at the Justice of the Peace the day after she found out that she was pregnant and have been together ever since.

Peter felt like he was the one who stopped his mother's dreams, and if she didn't "have responsibilities" she would have left his father many years ago.

Peter's father was a broken man who let alcohol rule his life. Peter told me he started drinking when his mother had a miscarriage with twins a couple of years back. That was five years ago, and he hadn't worked a day since.

As I entered Peter's room, I went straight to the bag that had the VGA2 gaming system. Peter sat beside me as I opened the bag.

"That's the VGA2. Where did you get that?"

"Fred and I got it in the city today."

"For real? That thing is mad expensive. Where did Fred get the money?"

I gave him a look because he knew that he had broken the unspoken rule, *"Keep your eyes on your fries."*

I smiled and said, "Let's set it up."

We opened the box excitedly. I could hardly control myself as I attached the wires to the back of his TV.

I hated reading the instructions for games and opted to get right to it. I popped in the game George sold me and started playing. That wasn't a great idea because I got destroyed in the first fifteen seconds on the first board.

Peter chuckled. "Read the instructions, dude."

The game instruction book reminded me of a mini textbook, and even though it was painful to read all those pages, I did. I must have been reading for a while because when I looked outside Peter's window, it was dark.

I looked at the clock on Peter's dresser and saw it was 7:30 p.m. My mother would be home in about a half an hour.

"Later, Peter," I said and jetted out of his apartment and into my building.

I ran up seven flights, and I had a couple more left when I saw Mr. Saks coming on his way down.

"Hello, Justin."

"Hello, Mr. Saks."

"I guess I am doing fine. Just that age has caught up to me. I don't move like I used to. I remember the good old days. Did you know that..."

I looked at my watch and said, "I got to go, Mr. Saks. I have homework to do."

"Well, in that case, young man, get to it. Education is very important. Very important."

That stopped Mr. Saks dead in his tracks. How predictable. That one statement made every adult in the world happy. They always wanted to hear that. Little did he know that I had no intention of doing any homework. I wanted to just chill out.

Mr. Saks always had tidbits of information which he called "Life's observations." I think he talked so much because he was lonely. I heard his wife had died ten years ago and his kids don't visit him anymore. I didn't blame them; he was old, grumpy, annoying and acted like a know-it-all. I didn't want to grow old and be like that. Plus he smelled like Ben-Gay and

Cheetos. A combination that would turn away human being off. Nasty!

When I got inside my apartment, I saw Albert sitting near the TV playing with his toys.

As soon as he spotted me, he yelled, "Cowabunga, Dude."

I smiled and got into a Teenage Mutant Ninja Turtle fighting stance and yelled, "Cowabunga, Dude."

He became excited and began laughing uncontrollably. Alicia was sitting on a small makeshift table near the kitchen area, still looking through the dictionary. As I approached her, I looked at piece of paper she had written a poem on.

Untitled
Life
Full of surprises
Expect the unexpected
Each day you awake
Search for the things that make you happy
Knowing that life appreciated is truly happiness enough

My sister wrote like a person twice her age, and I didn't want to tell her I actually thought she was smart. Her head was big enough.

I sat on the couch and watched a special on TV called *The Ridiculously Rich and Famous*. They were showcasing *celebrity pads*. One of these homes had twenty-five bedrooms, gold sinks, diamond studded door knobs—and a garage in the basement that held seventeen cars. I was trying to see what kind of cars were housed in there when I heard the phone ring.

I looked over to Alicia to get it, but she shot me back a stare that said, "I'm busy." I thought this was not worth the argument.

I answered on the second ring and heard the operator's nasal voice.

"Would you accept a collect call from Phillip Stanford?"

I hesitated because that was my father. He hadn't called in months, and every time he did he called collect.

I took in a deep breath and said, "I'll accept the charges."

I heard his deep voice. "Hello. Hello."

I wanted to hang up the phone, but I was curious to know what he wanted now.

"Yeah, Dad, it's me, Justin."

"How you doing, son?" he answered excitedly.

"Everything is fine, Dad. You know, Mama and the rest of us are just on the way to the theatre, and afterwards we are going down to Fifth Avenue and do some shopping. Do you want us to pick you up anything?"

His deep voice got louder. "You think everything is a joke. What is your problem? You better watch your tone, before I..."

I was furious; he had no right to tell me what to do all the way from Japan. "Before you what? You are no longer here, and we don't even know when you're coming back."

"I'll come when I can. Why are you giving me such a hard time, son?" he answered in a more subtle tone. "I just want to talk to you, Marcus, Albert, Alicia, and your mother. I miss you guys badly."

I wished my mother would divorce him, but I think she was still holding on to the idea of a nuclear family.

"Well, Dad, I have a headache; I'll let you speak to Alicia and Albert. Marcus is in the library, and Mama isn't back from work yet."

"Before you go, son. How is school? You bringing in those good grades? You know school is important."

This was becoming a subject matter that was sticking to me like a Siamese twin.

"School is alright, dad. I am handling my business."

"That's my boy. Get those A's. You'll need them in the real world. I want you to live out our namesake and be a Stanford going to and graduating from Stanford University."

What did my father know about school?

I had to prevent myself from laughing because my father dropped out of elementary school. He started as a janitor and made his way up the ranks. With his perseverance, focus, and hard work, he got to be CEO of a company in Manhattan that grossed billions of dollars every year. It took him twenty-two years, but he did it.

If he could do it, I could, too. His only mistake to me was his indulgence in alcohol and drugs.

"I'll let you speak to Alicia," I answered coldly.

I sat back on the couch and could tell that Alicia was happy to hear his voice. She was three years old when my father left. Albert wasn't born yet and only knew my father from pictures and hadn't actually had a face to face with him. Marcus remembered him a little bit.

I heard the door being pushed open, and I saw Marcus and my mother walking in. Alicia screamed that Dad was on the phone, and my mother didn't even take her coat off as she rushed to the phone.

"Hey baby, how you doing?"

I couldn't tell what they were saying, but I noticed tears rolling down her face. I went over to her, and she ushered me away.

"I'm okay, honey. It isn't that I am sad. Those are tears of joy. Honey, tears of joy."

Mama quickly went back to her conversation like I wasn't standing there and talked with my father another twenty minutes before handing Marcus the phone.

Mama seemed to have an infusion of energy.

"Justin, get that plastic bag I left by the door. We are having steak and lobster for dinner."

When someone ordered food in the restaurant and didn't want their order, my mother brought it home. That was the only time we ate like that. I was tired of her adding different things together and calling it a surprise: Beef Surprise, Chicken Surprise, Fish Surprise, and Turkey Surprise.

I was usually surprised, all right. Surprised that my stomach was still intact. When I ate her surprises, I'd think of Ms. Miles' cooking that was fit for kings and queens.

I enjoyed the steak and lobster along with the mashed potatoes and wished people would have taken back their orders every day.

It was getting late, and after I helped my mother wash the dishes, I went to my room and jumped up on the top bunk, hoping that Mr. Saks wouldn't go to the bathroom a lot that night.

I was in homeroom and looked to the front of the classroom and saw Roxanne. She was wearing another fly outfit, and I couldn't stop myself from staring. I was in a trance, and must have lost all my senses because as one of her friends passed by me she threw a little piece of balled up paper that landed in my mouth.

That woke me up from my trance, and I spit out the paper that almost went down the wrong pipe.

The bell rang and Roxanne made her way out of the classroom. "Keep your mouth closed. I know this is a sight to behold."

Roxanne slowed down right before she was out the door, turned around slowly, and winked at me.

That meant progress in my eyes.

I quickly made my way to history class and was bored as Mr. Goombaum began talking in his high pitched voice.

"There are seven continents in the world. Can anyone name them?"

Someone from the back of the classroom—I couldn't remember their name for the life of me—said, "Africa."

"Name another?"

"Antarctica," Theresa said as she rumbled through some papers on her desk.

"Good. Good. Any more."

Brandon who never answered questions in class said, "Asia."

"Keep it going, we have a couple more."

"Norttth Ammmerica," Betty stuttered.

"Name another."

"South America," Eduardo said as he began digging in his nose.

"Good, class. Can anyone name the last one?"

I needed the class participation points badly and decided to give it a try. I raised my hand and waved it like it was on fire.

Mr. Goombaum did a double take and said, "It's alive. It's alive. It has risen from the dead."

The class started laughing, but I kept my hand in the upright position.

"Okay, Justin. Let's see what you got."

"Oceanica."

Wesley, the smartest student in the class, blurted out, "What are you talking about, Justin? Mr. Goombaum said continents, not places or words you made up from your *imagination.*"

Wesley adjusted his collar on his neatly pressed dress shirt and said, "The answer is Australia, Mr. Goombaum."

"You are correct, Wesley."

Wesley looked at me in a way that said, *You are such an idiot.*

Mr. Goombaum added, "But so is Justin."

Wesley's smile turned into a frown.

Mr. Goombaum explained, "The word Oceania is also called Oceanica. A lot of different writers have used this term, and in several different languages this term is used to describe one of the continents. Australia. That also falls under New

Zealand, New Guinea, and various islands of the Malay Archipelago."

I had silently thanked Marcus because he had left some of his notes that he had written from some book he was reading next to the TV controller, and I had quickly glanced at it before moving his papers over to watch TV.

I looked back at Wesley and shook my head.

"Wesley, you need to read more. Don't you know that information is the key to knowledge?"

Wesley got upset when the class burst into laughter. I had to give him a taste of his own medicine; he used that same line on me last week when I insisted that Europe was separated into four hemispheres and not three.

My next class was uneventful, and I was looking forward to some kind of physical activity in my next class, which was gym. I hurriedly got dressed and came into the gymnasium. Everyone was playing basketball, and I thought, *Not today.* I was really uncomfortable playing basketball, but because of my height I was always picked to play.

When I lived in my old neighborhood, my favorite sport was tennis, and I had gotten pretty good at it. I had to give that up a while ago because, when I first moved to my new neighborhood and told them I was a tennis player, they informed me that tennis was a game for uppity people and no one in our neighborhood played that.

I got the picture when I realized that no one in my hood was walking around with tennis rackets [which are usually expensive] strapped to their backs. Plus, those non-baggy, tight white tennis shorts [which my mother always bought] weren't a good look either.

I had to try to fit in somehow, so I always played, even though I'd rather be watching. But my true reason was that all the girls liked watching the boys run up and down the court.

As the game started, I was in the middle playing the center position. They never passed me the ball, so I didn't shoot it much. I grabbed four straight rebounds on the offensive end, and, after our team quickly scored, I ran back down for defensive purposes. I got two blocks in a row and threw it down court for an easy lay up.

My team won three games in a row before my face was introduced to Max's elbow.

Max was short in height but built like a linebacker, and he had a bad attitude to match with his foul-smelling breath. I heard he had been getting arrested since he was seven and always repeated, "I am not afraid of anything, including death."

It was me and Max on a fast break. After I blocked his shot, he elbowed me in the nose on purpose because he said I was blocking too many shots and needed to be taught a lesson.

Blood started trickling down my nose, and I had to go to the nurse, who instructed me to keep my head elevated. I missed a period just trying to get the bleeding under control.

Things worked out better than I expected.

Thanks to Max, I didn't have to come up with an excuse for not having my homework for my next class. Matter of fact, I didn't do any homework for any of my classes. I could remain in the nurse's office all day, I thought.

The nurse seemed to catch onto my scheme. "You cannot stay in here all day for a nosebleed."

As I made my way to hygiene, I saw Roxanne again.

She walked up to me and said, "Your brother is Marcus, right?"

That was not how I had envisioned it would be; our first real meaningful conversation.

Roxanne was right in front of me, so close I could just steal a kiss and run for my life. I played it cool though and put my hand on the locker, like I had done it a million times before.

When I began answering her question, a little bit of spit flew out my mouth and landed on her right cheek.

Roxanne backed up, scrunched up her face in disgust, and said, "You are a walking mistake. Can't you control yourself?"

Why couldn't I get myself together? I put my head down in shame and walked away. I was such a dumpkoff! I was never going to get a chance with Roxanne.

As I made my way to lunch, I kept thinking about how cute Roxanne looked in her matching pink outfit and her sweet smelling perfume that reminded me of fresh roses.

I caught up with Peter, and we sat at the far end of the cafeteria where the loners "congregated," as Peter would say. This was always a good idea because Max and his friends loved to sneak up on unsuspecting victims and either smack them on their necks or smack them in their heads.

Before I put what resembled meat on my fork, I heard, "Bap, Bap, Bap."

Then a roar of laughter ensued, and I noticed Michael Freeman rubbing the back of his neck.

I didn't understand why Michael was so stubborn. He insisted on sitting in the same seat, and Max and his crew would slap him in the head every single day.

Michael was what the in-crowd called a "dorkus." He didn't really exist to anyone because he was always talking about weird things he read. People didn't know what he was talking about, and no one cared to find out what he was saying. I must admit, I didn't care either. It all seemed like a foreign language to me. He was a walking tape recorder. Every day he would be outside reciting some kind of statistic to himself.

* * *

Last month I had to sit next to him during a school trip to the museum.

Michael said, "Did you know an average high school dropout makes around $19,000?"

I answered, "Who cares?"

"Well, I do. I don't want to make $19,000 a year."

I had tried to look away, but he came with more statistics.

"Sixty-eight percent of all national prison inmates are high school dropouts. Did you also know that getting a Bachelor's degree, you can make over $2.1 million over an adult working life? With a Master's degree, $2.5 million, and with a doctoral degree you can make $3.4 million."

I shook my head and answered, "So what? I know some high school dropouts that made tons of money. I see them on TV all the time. Anything is possible if you believe."

"You are right. Anything is possible. But not everything is probable. I want to win not by chance but by increasing my chances for success. For everyone that makes it, there are millions that get swept under the rug."

Michael was going on about more statistics, but I welcomed the silence when Max, who was sitting behind us, interjected and said, "Shut up, you weirdo. No one wants to hear anything from you."

Michael became Sunday morning church service quiet and put his head down. Max leaned over the seat and smacked Michael in the head so hard I thought he was going to cry.

Michael shrieked in pain and began to call the attention of the school monitor, but put his hand down when Max put his two fingers together and ran it across his own neck slowly.

I was sick of hearing Michael talk as well, but I didn't like the way Max treated him. But I didn't want to take on a fight that wasn't any business of mine.

When I looked back at Max, he snarled and said, "What you looking at, Daddy Long Legs?"

The rest of the bus started laughing.

"Hey everyone, take a look," Max shouted. "Justin is a pitiful human being. Just tall for nothing. Long, lanky, and funny looking."

I hated to be embarrassed. I wanted to tell Max how his breath smelled so bad that it could raise the dead, but I had no backing on the bus. Peter couldn't fight his way out of a wet paper bag, and I didn't want to get jumped like Frank Morrison did on the first day of school.

* * *

It was sweet justice because a school aide caught Max slapping Michael and began escorting him out of the lunchroom. I heard him screaming, "What I do? What I do?"

"I saw what you did, young man. Hitting that boy like that. Are you crazy?"

"I didn't hit anyone," Max said, acting like he had no idea what the school aide was talking about.

"Yes, you did. I saw you."

Max became serious and wasn't giving up his point. "Ask him if I hit him."

"I don't have to ask anyone; I saw it with my own two eyes."

Max knew Michael wasn't going to say a word. I silently hoped that Max would be suspended again. That would be the third time this month. School was much safer when he wasn't around.

Peter was eating the meat like it was filet mignon. I just drank my chocolate milk and ate a piece of my banana. I was swallowing a bite when I noticed Roxanne and her girlfriends approaching.

I tried to look cool as they slowly walked towards our table. It appeared as if time was standing still as Roxanne seemed to float towards my direction. I quickly grabbed a napkin and wiped my mouth, paying attention to the corners. I didn't want any chocolate milk or banana evidence left.

Roxanne sat right in front of me. "What are you doing after school?"

I took a hard swallow.

"Well? What's up with you, the cat got your tongue?" Roxanne asked annoyed.

I started closing my eyes and reopening them.

One of her girlfriends looked puzzled and said, "What is his problem? Was he dropped on his head as a child?"

I began pointing to my mouth, and then began gagging.

Peter, who was sitting beside me, jumped into action and applied the Heimlich maneuver. He pumped my stomach one time, but I was still gagging.

Roxanne got up from the table and stood back. I was on full display. The whole cafeteria seemed to stopped moving and talking and began looking in my direction.

Peter pumped his fist in my midsection for the second time, and the small piece of banana came flying out of my mouth and landed right on Roxanne's white shirt, leaving a yellow stain.

Roxanne moved away in horror, mumbling something under her breath, and quickly made her way back to her table.

I was happy that Peter saved my life.

"Wow, Just. Roxanne has you all choked up," Peter said trying to stop himself from smiling.

I stared at him, and we laughed.

I sat back down and finished up my banana before leaving the lunchroom. The school aide had insisted that I go to the nurse to get checked out.

"Back again. You are quite the student. Are you accident prone or what?"

I tried ignoring her comments because I was feeling fine, but I wanted to milk this for as long as possible.

"I feel a little tired and just need to lay down for a while."

Ms. Fox took my blood pressure, pulse, and respiration then gave me a drink of water and replied, "You are fine. Just rest up in the room. For as long as you need."

That was music to my ears.

I took off my sneakers and relaxed on the ugly green and yellow couch in the back room.

Thirty minutes later, I heard Roxanne's angelic voice speaking to Ms. Fox. "Is Justin okay?"

"Yes, sugar. He is in there. But don't stay in there too long."

"Okay, I'll just be a minute."

As Roxanne walked in, the first thing I noticed was that stain mark on her white shirt.

Roxanne smiled at me and said, "Are you okay?"

"I think I'll be alright," I answered, possible hoping she would volunteer to be my personal nurse.

"I was wondering if I could come by your apartment today. Could you give me your address?"

"My address is..." I said, feeling proud of the fact that I had gotten out a full sentence without any mishaps.

"Would around 5:30 p.m. be good?"

"What would you like to do when you come over? Do you want me to cook you a meal or something?"

"You are so sweet. That would be great. I hope that won't be too much trouble."

"Oh, not at all. I'll just whip up a little something."

I knew that sounded corny, but everyone knows that a way to a person's heart is through their stomach.

My specialty was scrambled eggs and bacon, but that would have been lame. It was way past breakfast time, and if any of my siblings saw me cooking eggs and bacon, they would have put in their order as well. I sure wasn't trying to be a short order cook. *I'll call in a favor and order some food,* I thought.

I decided that I would stay in the nurse's office one more period. I got really comfortable and closed my eyes. I wanted to be all nice and rested for my big date.

It was finally time to go home, and I felt like the luckiest guy in the world. Actually, the world was too small for my feelings at that moment. I was the happiest guy in the universe.

I met up with Marcus, Alicia, Albert, and Peter outside of school.

"Come on, guys, we have to hurry up and get home."

"What's the rush?" Alicia said, looking at me strangely. "You never want to go straight home. You usually want to see if you can find your stupid friend, Fred."

I was in a good mood, and for once I didn't get into it with Alicia.

"I love you, Alicia. Life is good. Life is real good."

Alicia was dumbfounded, and Peter asked me if I was having an out of body experience or maybe that piece of banana mysteriously got stuck in my head and was affecting my brain.

I wanted to get home so quickly that I didn't even wait for red stoplights. I dodged a couple of cars in an intersection before we got to our apartment building.

Marcus, Alicia, and Albert decided to go to the library to get some books; after telling Peter, "Later," I jogged up the ten flights.

As soon as I got inside, I went to the bathroom and found some rubber gloves from under the sink. I cleaned the toilet bowl and scrubbed the bathtub and made sure everything was spic and span just like Ms. Miles would have done it.

I grabbed all the dirty towels that I had left on the floor in the morning and threw them in the hamper. Next was our small living room. I picked up every Teenage Mutant Ninja Turtle toy Albert had on the floor.

Then, I cleaned off the couch that had Alicia's dolls on it, and I went in the closet and sprayed some air freshener on the couch. That took care of the smell but the couch was still a horrendous sight. I went into the closet, found a big, long blanket my grandmother made, and covered the whole couch. It was just the touch it needed. It looked a lot better for company.

Then, I ran to the closet and took out what my mother called the "dirt-dusting machine." It was like having a vacuum cleaner only that it wasn't motorized.

I went over the carpet a couple of times and had to keep going back to the garbage to dump all the dust that was stuck in it. This contraception had its limitations because it couldn't pick up the big items. I had to get on my hands and knees and pulled up cereal, paper clips, and coins.

Next, I went into our kitchen area and started washing all the dishes. I was supposed to do that last night, but I was tired. It took me a while to get the stains out of the cereal bowls and especially the lasagna that was stuck to the plates. The glasses took forever because they were stained with cherry Kool-Aid. I cleaned off the stove and wiped down our small counter.

I went to my room and began dusting and made sure to make my bed. I never made my bed unless my mother got on my case. What was the point? I was going to be getting back into it anyway. But maybe today Roxanne would like to sit on it with me, I thought.

I didn't want to do it, but I made Marcus's and Alicia's beds, and that made the room look presentable.

I surveyed everything—bathroom, kitchen, living room—and could only remember the apartment being that clean on Christmas, which was the one day of the year Mama didn't work.

I grabbed the telephone book and looked up Russiani's. It was across town, and they never delivered to our area because they were afraid that they might get robbed.

My cousin Earl worked there part time. I dialed their number, and the receptionist answered on the first ring.

"Hello, is Earl there?"

"Who may I say is speaking?

"Justin."

"Please hold."

Russiani's was the restaurant our family would go to every Wednesday night when we lived in Selden. We would order lobster, steak, fish, and every other delicacy from the menu.

As an hors d'oeuvre, I always had caviar. Marcus and Alicia didn't recall too much of that because they were younger, but I remembered it like it was yesterday.

"What's up, cousin?" I said as I recognized Earl's voice.

"Can't call it. How's the hood treating you?"

"Doing what I got to do."

"When you coming back to the old neighborhood?"

"Soon. Very soon," I lied. "I need the hook up on some food. When do you get off?"

"In twenty minutes."

"Alright then. Get me some steak, lasagna, lobster, French fries, caviar—"

"Are you crazy? How I am going to swing that?"

How quickly people forget. My cousin had owed me big for not telling his mother that he had wrecked her 1950 Porsche when he could hardly see over the steering wheel.

"Do you remember a certain vehicle on a certain date—"

"Alright alright. I'll just take it out of my check. This blackmail thing is getting old, though."

"I won't ask you again. Don't worry." I snickered. "Sike. You'll be paying until we are senior citizens."

The phone went silent, and I had to say hello a couple of times before Earl responded.

"I'll be there in a half an hour. Be outside. I don't want to be in your neighborhood at night time."

"You punk," I laughed. "Are you a man or a mouse?"

"Whatever. Make sure you are outside."

I hung up the phone, went to the bathroom, and quickly showered.

I went to my Mama's room and looked under her bed and found remnants of my father. I grabbed some of his cologne and sprayed behind my ears, on my wrists, and on my chest. I wanted to smell as appealing as possible.

I decided to take out my best outfit, which was my silk shirt and gray slacks, and I went back to the closet and took out my black shoes, grabbed the shiner, and buffed my shoes until I could see my own reflection.

It was 4:10 when I heard the horn honking outside. I went downstairs and picked up the food. Earl looked so scared. He almost hit a cat that was slowly waltzing across the street as he sped off.

I ran back upstairs and put some pots in the sink and covered it with a towel so Roxanne would believe that I did all the cooking.

I knew my siblings would be back any minute, and I wanted to make sure they had all eaten before Roxanne arrived. Alicia was the first one through the door.

"What is going on here? This apartment is cleaner than a hospital. Did Mama come home and clean?"

"No, stupid," I barked. "I decided to just clean up a little."

She put her hands on her hips. "Oh really. So why do you have on your so called "playa" outfit? The last time I saw that thing was when you were trying to impress Suzy Thompson at Sunday school."

That was not a pleasant experience. When I went to profess my love, her boyfriend, who I didn't even know existed, informed me that if I spoke to her again I would end up in a wheelchair.

This didn't seem too farfetched because dude looked like he was on steroids, and I was not trying to be his punching bag.

Marcus came in next and began sniffing the air.

"That smells like lasagna. Did Mama get food from the restaurant?"

"Nah. I got us some stuff from Russiani's."

Alicia chimed in, "Where did you get Russiani's money? I hope you're not stealing."

"Alicia, you are working my last nerve. Of course I wouldn't do something that stupid. Just sit down and eat."

I grabbed the knives and forks, and everyone was seated. Albert began clapping as I came to the table.

"French fries and a cheeseburger. My favorite."

I wished my mother was home; she would have loved this spread. I even missed my father. But I wasn't going to get all depressed. I needed to be focused for Foxy, Roxy.

I told my siblings I wasn't hungry and just watched them enjoy their food. I began looking at my watch, and Alicia spotted me.

"Do you have a date?"

"Eat your food and shut up."

"Let me put this all together. Clean house. Expensive food. Your best outfit. Cologne. And you even used Listerine for your stank breath."

"So what? I am having company, and I want you guys to be on your best behavior."

"What crazy girl would want you? Yuck."

I was sick of her mouth. "Roxanne Fletcher."

Alicia laughed so hard that she almost fell out of her chair.

"Alicia, stop it," Marcus said. "Cut Justin a break. Before I tell that boy you like in school tomorrow that you sometimes pee on your bed."

Alicia became quiet and went back to eating her food.

Marcus looked at Alicia and said, "It is true. Roxanne Fletcher is coming here. I believe at 5:30. That is what she told me in the hallway before eighth period. I am going to be helping her with some math equations. She wants to take advanced math next year."

"What are you talking about? Roxanne is coming to see me," I said, as I handed Albert a napkin to wipe his dirty mouth.

"Slow down, bro. I don't want her. It's just work. I have my mind on the future. There will be plenty of time for girls later on. Education is my girl. And speaking of that, she needs some attention. Let me get my math book. Roxanne doesn't know a fraction from a subtraction sign."

I turned on the TV and sat and watched a comedy show; before long, I heard the bell ring.

I jumped up and quickly went to the door and looked through the peephole.

It was Roxanne, and as I opened the door I smelled her flowery perfume. She leaned in and kissed me on the left cheek then on the right cheek.

"That is how they do it in France. I would love to go there some day. You know how many "hot" outfits I can buy and places I could explore? Their food, architecture, everything. I better take some French lessons."

I stood paralyzed still thinking about the fact that her lips touched my skin.

"Are you going to stand in the doorway, or are you going to let me in?"

I let her in and closed the door behind her.

"Are you hungry?"

"Nah. I ate already."

I had gone to all that trouble for the food, and she didn't want to eat. What was that all about?

Roxanne sat down on the couch and looked around, taking in her surroundings as if she were a social worker.

"My apartment looks just like yours, but I don't have any siblings. I kind of have the apartment to myself because since my father died my mother hasn't been in the apartment too often. Most of the time she stays in the Bronx with her half sister."

"It must be lonely."

"Me lonely? I could have company anytime I want and as long as my mother sends the money for the rent. I'm good. It is like having my own pad."

As she sat on the couch she crossed her legs like a real lady, and the baby oil she put on her legs glistened from the ceiling light.

I began having a brain freeze and couldn't think of anything else to say. The silence was nerve wracking.

Roxanne played with her hair, nervously twirling it around her index finger. "Where is your brother? He said he would help me with some math problems. I don't want to be here all night."

My dream date was officially shattered into a million pieces. Marcus was right. Roxanne wasn't here to really see me at all. I wanted to crawl under a rock.

My silk shirt began feeling like poison ivy and I began itching all over. I composed myself and pointed to the closed door. Roxanne knocked, went inside, and closed it behind her.

For the first time in my life, I wished I was smarter. I wanted to be my brother. But I knew it wasn't possible. Roxanne wasn't feeling me at all. I realized that I didn't have anything to offer her.

I was feeling down in the dumps and went to the closet, took off my outfit, put on my sweatshirt and corduroy pants, and went to the phone.

The phone rang three times before Peter answered.

"Can I come over?"

"Bet. Hurry up. My mom will be coming home from work soon."

I peeked inside my mother's room, where I saw Alicia and Albert fast asleep. This was a relief. If Alicia was up and found out I was going out, I would have had to pay her to keep her mouth shut.

Before I knocked on my room door, I gently pressed my ear against it. I heard my brother and Roxanne laughing.

I knocked, and they instantly became quiet.

Marcus yelled, "Come in."

I opened the door and wondered why Roxanne had to be so close to him to learn math.

"I'm going to Peter's. Watch Alicia and Albert for me. I'll be back in an hour or two."

During the whole time I spoke to Marcus, Roxanne didn't look in my direction once. Her head was buried in the textbook.

I made a quick exit and didn't even say goodbye as I closed the door.

Ten seconds later, I heard them laughing again, and wanted to know what was so funny.

Marcus was the corniest guy in the world. His jokes were drier than sandpaper.

I pressed my ear against the door again, and I heard him telling his favorite joke. "Hey Roxanne. Do you want to hear a dirty joke?"

"Okay. Let's hear."

"A white cow fell into the mud."

Roxanne began giggling uncontrollably and my brother joined in. What horrible sounds. They sounded like a cross between a dolphin and a hyena.

I was officially through.

After a glass of cherry Kool-Aid, I left the apartment.

Peter's elevator was out. Great! I slowly made my way up the eleven flights to his apartment.

As soon as I got inside, I asked for something to drink, and he gave me a large glass of lemonade.

Peter's father was passed out on the couch, and was snoring so hard I first thought that a train was passing through the apartment.

We went into Peter's room and began playing a boxing game for the VGA2. I took out all my frustrations on Peter. I was knocking Peter down with the one-two [right-left] combo followed with an uppercut.

Peter was defenseless because he never quite got the idea that you had to block when someone else was throwing a punch.

It was amazing how some games mirror real life. The fights Peter got into, he never blocked either, and he had amassed quite a few black eyes as a result.

We played until it was dark.

I left his apartment, and decided to take a stroll around the neighborhood.

The moon was out, and I wished I were in the sky with the stars. Anything would have felt better than how I was feeling at the moment. I walked a couple of blocks before noticing that my left shoelace was dragging on the ground. I went to tie my shoelace when I noticed a shadow approaching me.

Before I could turn around, someone was poking me in my side with a hard object. "Don't move or it's a Reynolds. Empty your pockets NOW."

"Don't kill me," I squeaked. "I don't have any money. Please don't kill me."

"Well, too bad. Get on your knees."

I began weeping and started praying out loud.

The stranger started laughing and said, "Open your eyes. It's me, Fred. Don't wet your pants. I thought you said that you don't believe in prayer. You sure seemed to be praying real hard."

I wiped my eyes and was so happy it was someone I knew, I began hugging him.

"Chill. Chill. What if someone sees us? Keep it together. I told you not to be out here late at night. I have been following you for a couple of blocks. You didn't turn around once, and you busy staring at the stars like you are an astronomer or something. Don't get caught slipping."

"I thought you were still in jail."

"Nah. They had to let me go. The only strong evidence they had on me, they broke. I talked about that officer's wife on the way to the station, and he got so agitated that he threw the tape at me. How stupid. I dodged it, and it hit the back window. When I was in the station, they had me in this small room questioning me about jumping the turnstile. Their only chance was for me to tell on myself. He knew that I had to confess, and I played dumb and told him I don't know what they were talking about and I wanted my lawyer to be present. I didn't say another word. My lawyer came in a little bit later, and the rest they say is history."

I scratched my head. Fred knew the law better than some lawyers, and he reminded me that he had a photographic memory; once he sees something, it sticks inside his head like a rat stuck on a glue trap.

"Let me walk you to your building. You can never be too sure."

I walked beside Fred and noticed another new outfit with sneakers and hat to match. I reminded myself, the next time I saw him I would ask him to teach me how to get that paper and stay fresh to death. Maybe that would help me to impress Roxanne, I thought.

It must have been a miracle because the elevator was working, and I quickly got upstairs to my apartment.

As I got off, I saw Mr. Saks.

"Hey, young fellow," he said as he slowly came down the stairs. "Do you have a minute?"

I quickly answered, "No, I don't. I have to get inside and do my homework."

"Very good, young man. You are very dedicated to your future. I'll speak to you another time. Have a good night."

That stopped him dead in his tracks again. Education was such an Achilles' heel for most adults. It was like a Get Out of Jail Free card.

As I approached my apartment door, I heard Roxanne's laugh. *What is she still doing here?* It was almost 10:30.

As I opened the door, Roxanne was on the couch sitting next to Marcus and watching TV.

Roxanne said, "Hey Justin. You didn't tell me your brother was so charming."

I looked over at Marcus, and he was smiling like he was taking school photos.

"He is a regular Prince Charming."

I looked into Mama's room, and Alicia and Albert were still asleep. I went to the refrigerator and noticed someone made more Kool-Aid, but there wasn't enough left to fill half a glass. I was in no mood to make any, so I drank tap water and headed to the couch.

I went to sit down, but they both gave me the look that said I should get lost. I got the hint loud and clear and went to my room, jumped up to the top bunk, and just stared at the ceiling.

I must have dozed off because I turned over to see Marcus shaking me. "I am going to walk Roxanne home. I'll be back soon."

I wiped my eyes and decided to pull the big brother card.

"It is almost midnight. You are my responsibility. I'll walk her home. Just stay put."

Marcus stared down at his feet, and I knew that meant we were going to have an argument.

He came close to my ear and said, "No way. I am going to walk her home. If you are so worried, you can tag along, but you can't make me."

My brother was really flexing on me.

"Over my dead body will you be leaving this house alone."

"I am going. And matter of fact I am going by myself, or I will be telling Mama about you having your friends over on a school night," Marcus said with a devilish smile on his face.

I was furious. This blackmailing thing was getting old, but I knew Mama would have my head, and it was not worth the drama over a girl who wasn't feeling me anyway.

"Alright. Do whatever."

Marcus left, and ten minutes later I heard a knock on the door.

"Come in," I shouted.

The door opened slowly and a sweet smell of perfume took over the room. I quickly popped up in an upright position with my legs dangling down from the top bunk.

"I just wanted to say that I was leaving. Thank you for having food for me. Maybe I'll see you around in school," Roxanne said. "Would you mind walking with us? It's late, and I know you will protect me and your brother if anything were to happen."

I wanted to tell her to go jump in the river, but after she showed me her pearly whites I answered, "Sure. Let me get my sneakers."

As we got outside, I felt the chill of night, and my brother beat me to the punch by offering Roxanne his jacket.

Roxanne looked at my brother and said, "You are so sweet. What a gentleman, and the smartest boy in the school. I can tell you are going places."

I walked a couple of steps behind them because it was almost like I wasn't even there. It was really a frigid night, and I looked around in every direction, trying to make sure no one snuck up on us. It was about a twenty-block walk, but we finally reached her apartment building.

Roxanne's building was newer than ours, and you could tell that their superintendent did what he was supposed to. Marcus walked her up to the double doors in front of her building. Roxanne gave Marcus a big hug and kissed him on his left cheek, right cheek, then on his forehead.

That should have been me, but what did I have to offer Roxanne right now? Absolutely nothing.

It was dark, but I could still see my brother blushing and giggling like a five-year-old girl. Roxanne must have thought that was cute and giggled along with him. Then they began talking, but I couldn't quite make out what they were saying.

I should have practiced when Fred was trying to teach me how to read lips. What I did remember was that the key was to be as close as possible, which wasn't an option for me, so I abandoned that idea.

Before Roxanne went into her building, she waved from a distance and said, "Later, Justin."

My brother got a hug, multiple kisses, and I got a "later."

As Marcus and I walked back home I realized how happy he was. He was practically skipping along.

"Wouldn't you say tonight is a dazzling night. Have you noticed it is a full moon? How beautiful? How romantic. There is something special in the air tonight," Marcus said. "Anyway, Roxanne is pretty cool, and a looker, as well."

"A looker, huh? I thought you said you don't have time for girls. You are all about your education."

"Of course, bro. But I am not blind. Roxanne is a babe, but I have more pressing things on my mind."

"Like what?"

"Like college. I want to attend, and how I am going to pay for it? I've been researching scholarships, and I want to take some advanced summer classes so I can get college credits before I even enter college."

"You have your life all planned out. Don't you?"

"Well, not really. I don't know what obstacles will be placed ahead of me. But I do know that I have goals, and that is what I will focus on. Without goals, you can't be successful."

I wanted to hurl because that was like something a teacher, Mama, Dad, or Mr. Saks would say.

"You know what I mean, right?" Marcus asked.

"Sure. I have one goal."

"What goal is that?"

"Getting money, and getting a whole lot of it."

"Money isn't everything."

"Are you crazy? Money is power. I don't know how I'll get it right now, but it is going to happen, and I won't have to go to college at all."

We arrived at our building and got into bed ten minutes before Mama arrived. As I sat staring at the ceiling, something dawned on me. I had left Alicia and Albert in the apartment by themselves for the second time. I was slipping. Roxanne had my mind all twisted. Thank goodness nothing happened to them.

Surprisingly, I had finally gotten a really good night's sleep [thanks to Mr. Saks, who had probably passed away in his sleep, because I didn't hear the toilet flush once last night].

I quickly got up and headed to the bathroom. Marcus was already inside, and I heard his awful rendition of Michael Jackson.

"The way you make me feel. You knock me off of my feet now baby."

My brother singing loves songs. He has been officially bitten by the Roxanne bug.

I knocked on the door and shouted, "Hurry up, lover boy. I don't want to be late for school."

I must have been louder than usual because, as I banged the second time, my mother came out of her room.

"What is all that noise about? I am trying to get some sleep."

I was startled. "Sorry, Mama. How come you are not at work?"

"I called in sick. I have a pain in my knee that just won't go away."

I could tell by Mama's face that she was in severe pain. My mother hadn't missed a day of work in five years. Through snow, sleet, rain, she was there.

Marcus came out of the shower, and I went in, quickly showered, and got dressed. Alicia and Albert were eating cereal while Marcus was reading a new book.

I went over to my mother and said, "Mama, you should really get that checked out. I'll go with you to the hospital today."

"Honey. That is sweet. But you know we don't have health insurance, and I have no money to spare."

I looked over to Marcus. If he didn't want all those books, we would have some extra money.

"Mama, I'll call Uncle Paul," I said, as I handed her a cup of coffee.

Uncle Paul was my father's brother and cousin Earl's father. He was a general practitioner and had his own private practice in Manhattan. We were pretty cool; last time I saw him, he told me, if we needed anything I shouldn't hesitate to call.

I searched for his cell number in my room and got him right before he was going through the door for work that morning. It took some convincing, but he said he would pick us up in front of our building.

My other siblings went to school as I stood outside with Mama waiting for Uncle Paul.

I could hardly hear the engine purr as it came around the corner. His car was off the hook. He drove a chocolate brown Rolls Royce Phantom that was showroom clean.

As I opened the back door, which opened reversely [like two refrigerator doors], and sat down in its plush eggshell color interior, I felt like I had died and gone to heaven.

A tray came down off the back seat like when you are on an airplane, and I stretched out my legs comfortably with quite a bit of space to spare.

I played with his laptop computer, surfing the Internet as we drove along.

Mama didn't really like Uncle Paul because she felt that Dad was always trying to keep up with him, and it was through Uncle Paul's friends that he started to make the wrong decisions.

I wasn't trying to take sides because my auntie told me that Uncle Paul tried to warn him initially. My auntie called my father "hard headed" and that Uncle Paul didn't have to look out for him because he was the older one and could take care of himself.

Everyone in the neighborhood was trying to see who was driving the car, but since it had the dark tinted windows you couldn't tell who was in there.

If I had a car like that, I wouldn't have tinted windows. That way everyone could see it was me.

"So, Uncle, when did you get this?"

"I got it last week. What do you think?"

"Three letters: H O T."

He laughed. "Well, nephew. Work hard. Play hard. That is what school has done for me."

Now this conversation was sounded like an infomercial about school. I knew it would be coming. It was just a matter of time.

A couple of seconds later, "How are you doing in school? Bringing home those A's?"

"Something like that. I'm doing what I have to do."

"Good. You already know why school is important —."

My mother interrupted. "He sure does. Isn't that right, baby?"

"I sure do."

Truth be told, I hadn't shown my mother my real report card all year long. She hadn't been able to come to the parent-teacher meetings because she worked all the time. I had this boy in school make up a fake report card, and I only gave it to her when she really pressed me.

After changing the topic, I continued asking my uncle about all the features the car had to offer and asked him could I drive it when I was old enough.

He smiled and said, "If I still have it. I get bored of these things. I'll be upgrading when the newer model comes out. What do you teenagers call it again?"

"Fresh to death, Uncle."

"Oh yes. Fresh to death. I love being fresh to death."

When we got inside his office, my uncle immediately started examining my mother. Taking her blood pressure...a full examination.

He started feeling around her knee and she howled in pain.

Uncle Paul looked up and said, "We have to take some x-rays, and I'll get back to you with the results in a couple of days."

Mama and I took the train home even though Uncle Paul had tried to pay for a cab. Mama was so proud. I would have said something, but I understood it took a lot for her to go to any doctor in the first place.

When we got to our apartment, Mama went back in her room because she was complaining of stiffness in her knee. I had the rest of the day to myself and sat on the couch watching TV until my siblings came home.

I'd been cooped up in the apartment most of the day and told Marcus to watch everyone while I went to Peter's house. I was playing video games for hours, and Peter was still no match for me in the boxing game. It was like challenging a man on foot to a race with a motorcycle. Victory was pretty much guaranteed.

Peter didn't want to give up. I got to give it to him, he was sure persistent. I asked him if he had enough, but he responded, "Persistence is stronger than resistance."

He started the game up again and we played until it was dark outside.

As I exited his building I saw Fred walking around the corner. I noticed he had his headphones on, and I silently snuck up behind him and pointed two fingers together as hard as I could into his side.

Fred stood still in his tracks.

"Don't turn around, or you are going to be taking a dirt nap. Give me your money," I demanded.

Fred said in the calmest voice I've ever heard, "You are going to have to kill me. Because I am not giving up nothing!"

I turned Fred around, and he saw my face.

"Fred, you would have really died here today?"

"No one is going to take anything from me. I would rather die than give up my stuff. If word gets around that I was ever robbed then every other chump will try me. I have a reputation to uphold!"

We walked to my building; before I went inside, Fred went into his backpack.

"A friend owes me a favor. So he gave me nine new video games for the VGA2. I know you like these things."

I gave him a pound and remembered that if Alicia or Marcus saw these games, I would have to answer a lot of questions.

I went back to Peter's apartment, and told him to hold them for me and I would see him tomorrow. We chuckled as we heard his father snoring up a storm.

As I sat in homeroom, I saw Roxanne looking good as usual. Roxanne and her friends smiled at me when they noticed I was staring in their direction. They all said in unison, "Hi, Justin."

What was happening? Did I miss something? Even Brandon had the look on his face that said, *How did he pull that one off?*

I answered in my sexiest voice, "Hi, ladies."

The homeroom bell rang. When Roxanne's friends passed me, they asked me if I minded if they came over tonight to go over some math work with Marcus.

They informed me that they had already spoken to Marcus, and he wanted to make sure it was okay with me. I was annoyed, and even though I wanted to tell them to take a long walk off a short pier, maybe I could convince them to speak to Roxanne on my behalf.

"Sure, ladies. You can come over today. Do any of you guys want dinner?"

All three girls answered in unison.

"That would be nice."

The day zoomed by. Before I knew it, Roxanne's friends were at the door. They all greeted me with a firm handshake. After they gobbled down the food I had gotten from Russiani's, they made their way to my room.

I heard a lot of giggling and laughing, and Marcus told his white-cow-in-the-mud joke again. At his punch line, the laughter ensued, and I wanted to be in the room to hang out with them as well and maybe impress them so they could tell Roxanne what a cool dude I really was.

After hours of intense math practice, they exited the room and made their way to the door. Marcus received three kisses on the cheek and three hugs as they hurriedly exited our apartment.

My window of opportunity was officially closed, and they didn't even bother to thank me for the food I provided. How rude!

I was mentally exhausted and fell asleep right before midnight.

It was Saturday, and I was happy that I didn't have to go to school. I woke up around 10:30 even though I wanted to stay in bed longer. Mr. Saks woke me up again last night, and I realized he was definitely alive.

When you get old, your bladder must be very weak. What would have been a solution to all my problems was if he bought a bedpan or even peed in a bottle or if he just wore some diapers.

I went into the living room and saw Roxanne. I rubbed my eyes a couple of times to make sure I wasn't dreaming.

Marcus was sitting on the couch with Roxanne next to him, watching TV. Albert was sitting on her lap, and Alicia was playing with her hair.

"Good morning, everyone," I said.

Everyone looked at me and responded, "Good morning, Justin."

"Hey, Roxanne. What are you doing here?"

"Trying to get this math thing together."

There was no reason for me to stick around, so I jumped into the shower, got dressed, and went to Peter's.

Peter's father was in his usual spot with the remote control stuck to his hand, and Peter reminded me that he hardly watched the TV; most of the time the TV watched him.

I played video games for seven hours straight and left fifteen minutes before Peter's mother came home from work.

As I entered my building, I saw Roxanne coming down the stairs.

"Hey, Justin. Do you mind walking me home?"

"Why don't you ask my brother? You didn't come to see me."

Roxanne came so close to me I got goose bumps.

"Please. It's late. Don't act like that," she said as she batted her *PERFECT* eyelashes.

I was under her control. I couldn't resist. Roxanne was looking and smelling angelic.

"Okay."

As we walked the twenty blocks, Roxanne was pretty quiet. I was as well because I was trying to keep my eye out for anybody sneaking up on us.

When we got in front of her building, Roxanne gave me a hug and a kiss on the cheek and said, "You're sweet. But I don't know about you."

"What do you mean?" I answered still thinking about her lips touching my skin again.

"I mean, I don't know if you are going places."

I was upset. "You mean going places like my brother."

"Are you jealous? Your brother is way too young. Plus he made it clear that he has goals and he is not going to let anyone interfere with that. I respect that a lot. A boy with plans."

I felt relieved, and that meant I still had a shot with Roxanne.

Roxanne looked me straight in my eyes and asked, "Do you have plans? Do you know what you want out of life?"

I blurted out, "I want money. Isn't that what everyone wants?"

"I don't know. Sometimes I think, heck yeah, and other times I think, nah," she said as she twirled her hair. "I am going inside. Thanks for the walk home. I'll see you in school on Monday."

It was Sunday morning, and I was happy that my mother wasn't home. That meant that I didn't have to go to church. No matter what, Marcus, Alicia, and Albert went every Sunday. It wasn't worth a drop of my time. I tried to keep myself occupied by finding other things to pass my time.

I was on my way out the door when the phone rang.

I hurried back to answer it.

"This is the operator. I have a collect call from Phillip Stanford. Will you accept the charges?"

"Yes. I'll accept the charges."

"Hello. Hello."

I answered in a short manner, "It's me, Justin. Dad, what's up?"

"Son, it is good to hear your voice."

"Oh really? When you coming home? Do you know how many years you've been gone?"

"I know, son. I am working on some things. I will go home soon."

"If I had a dollar for every time you said that. Not only would we be rich. We wouldn't have to live in this crummy apartment."

"Look, son. Why are giving me such a hard time?"

"Are you kidding me? We are the ones that have it hard."

My father quickly changed the subject, "Is your mother there? What about Alicia, Albert, or Marcus?"

"Mama is at work. And everyone else is at church."

"What are you doing home?"

I was sick of explaining myself to him. How dare he question me so many miles away. I didn't respond, I just hung up the phone.

The phone rang another three times, but I decided I wasn't going to pick it up. For what?

I left and went to Peter's apartment.

I was having a great time playing each of the new videogames Fred got me. And even though Peter stunk in video games, it was fun having him around.

Peter finally got frustrated from the whooping I was handing out and said he quit.

Peter got up, went to his desk, and began drawing me playing video games in his room with all of them scattered on the floor. He told me he would add the details and effects later on to really make it look more realistic.

Peter drew like it was the easiest thing to do in the world. He was truly gifted. I could see him being a professional illustrator one day.

Around 6:00, I left Peter's apartment and went back home. My siblings were all home, and Marcus's head was buried in his books as usual. Albert was practicing his two-times tables aloud. I went over to Alicia, who was putting on some finishing touches on one of her poems:

<u>My Mission</u>
I want to touch lives
Make the world a better place
No matter the ethnicity or race
Fight for what is right
Defend those who have no voice
Keep learning that we have to live together in this place.

My mother came in around 8:30. When I saw that brown plastic bag in her arms, I knew that we were having leftovers.

We ate steak and vegetables, and afterwards we all sat on the couch watching an animated movie until the phone rang.

My mother jumped up to answer the phone.

"Yes, I will accept the charges."

I knew I was going to be in trouble. I quickly made up an excuse that I had a headache and that I was going to bed.

I knew it wasn't going to be that easy, and I heard my mother call me into her room about thirty minutes later.

"Justin. Don't you ever disrespect your father like that again," she said in her sternest voice. "Are we 100 percent clear?"

I put my head down and said, "Yes, ma'am. But—"

"But nothing. It is hard on all of us, baby. But you need to learn how to forgive and understand that everyone is a work in progress."

I didn't understand why Mama was so understanding. We were hardly making ends meet, and my father hadn't sent a penny in five years.

I went back to bed and couldn't fall asleep because Mr. Saks was peeing again.

I was up again at 3:30 in the morning thanks to Mr. Saks. He was like a leaky faucet. I wanted to turn him off for good.

I couldn't fall back asleep, so I went into the living room and turned on the TV. I was amped when the commercial for the VGA2 came on; I felt honored to have one.

At the end of the commercial, they talked about a new video game called *Tai Chi Reign* that wasn't set to come out in the United States until next month.

My mother got up around 4:15, and I put on the kettle and made her a cup of coffee.

My mother hobbled as she left the apartment, and that reminded me that I would have to call Uncle Paul sometime in the week to talk about the test results on her knee.

I saw Roxanne in the hallway, and she smiled at me again. I was beholding her beauty [thinking how she lit up any space she occupied] but was distracted by the sudden stinging sensation I felt on the back of my neck.

I turned around and saw Max.

He was back again, and I wished he wasn't in school. "What's up, Daddy Long Legs? Look at your pants. Is there a flood? Your sneakers are mad dirty. Were you working in a pigpen?"

Everyone in the hallway started laughing. Anger started boiling up inside me, and I just exploded.

I gave Max a one-two [left-right] combo, followed up with a left uppercut just like I was playing the VGA2 boxing game. Max hit the ground like he was standing on a rug that got pulled from under his feet.

Max's friends came running to his aide. One tried to hit me. I dodged his left and gave him a right cross. His other friend saw his friend hit the ground, looked at me with my fists balled up, and just ran in the other direction.

Everyone was shocked, and I realized what I had done when the security guard grabbed me by the neck and escorted me to the Principal's office.

Max and his friends were in the office too. When Principal Frank questioned them, they remained silent.

"So no one has anything to say, huh?"

We all still remained as quiet as church mice.

"Well, Justin, since no one is talking and several people in the hallway, including two teachers, said you were the aggressor and that you threw an onslaught of punches," Principal Frank said as he fiddled with the stapler that was on his desk, "you will be suspended for a month."

I answered nervously, "But...but..."

Principal Frank was disgusted. "You are lucky I don't suspend you for two months. You are really out of control."

Principal Frank grabbed my folder out of his cabinet and said, "You really need a time out. You are on the road to repeating the eighth grade. Don't you care? What do you want out of life?"

He turned to Max and told him and his friends to go back to class and that he had his eyes on them because they were also on the verge of repeating the eighth grade.

As I left the office, I realized I was in deep trouble.

Now Mama had to be notified, and that's when the truth was going to be revealed.

My cutting. My grades.

Most of all, how was I going to handle Max and his friends when they saw me around the way?

After an hour of sitting outside the Principal's office, I saw my mother hobbling into the main office.

She momentarily glanced at me as she went into Principal Frank's office. An hour later, she came out and told me we were going home.

On the way home, she didn't say one word to me or even look in my direction.

When we got inside our apartment, she went to the closet, got a small suitcase, and stuffed in some of my belongings.

She took a piece of paper from her purse—my report card—and handed it to me.

"So this is what you have been doing at school. I work hard to put food on the table and work all these shifts. I trust you to be responsible, and this is how you repay me."

I didn't feel like I let her down at all. "Mama, I hate school. I hate this apartment. I hate that Dad isn't here. I hate that we don't have money like we used to. I hate my life. We need more money."

"You just don't get it. Do you think money will solve everything?" she said, holding back her tears.

"Yes, I do Mama. Yes, I really do."

"I have already talked to your Uncle Paul, and he said you can stay with him for a month. I'll give you a month to get your act together. I can't deal with you right now. I will not have you affecting your brothers and sister. They see the importance of education. You, on the other hand, really don't get it."

It was a welcoming sound when the phone rang and my uncle told me to meet him outside. I wanted to hug my mother badly, but I could tell she was not in the mood.

As we drove to his home in Selden, New York, I just fell asleep. The only thing I was truly missing at that moment was my VGA2. But strangely enough, I thought about Alicia and all her wisecracks, too. *I must be tired; that girl gets on my last nerve.*

It was about a forty-five minute ride to Selden from where we lived, and I was happy when we finally got there.

Uncle Paul's house was "off the Richter scale." [That's what Marcus would have said.]

I still didn't quite know what that meant, but he always used it to describe something really hot.

Actually, the whole neighborhood was a vision to behold, like where we used to live a couple of towns away.

I went inside and put my things in the room next to cousin Earl's.

Earl was seventeen, finishing up his last year of high school, and got accepted to all the Ivy League schools. He wasn't quite sure where he was going, but he told me wherever he landed would be a calculated decision—most importantly, a family decision.

Uncle Paul knocked on the door as I began putting my few belongings in the closet.

"The rules are quite simple. Be in the house by 6:00 p.m. and don't have any uninvited guests," Uncle Paul said, pointing his finger in my direction. "Any questions?"

Before I could answer, he closed the door.

At 6:00, Earl called me down for dinner.

As we sat at the table, I realized how much I missed this lifestyle. My uncle's wife, Ms. Clara as she told us to call her, had bad taste. Her color schemes were all off: Bearskin rugs, yellow walls, polka dot lamps, red carpeting, cheetah print pillows on the couch, modern and antique furniture in the same room, and a hot pink grand piano.

Ms. Clara spent most of her time watching the Home Shopping Network. Whatever they said was the newest style on TV, she would order it and have it delivered the next day.

Uncle Paul told me on the way up that one of the things he wanted me to do was clean out the basement and the garage and sort out all the piling junk that was forming in both places.

My other cousin Fredricka was home from school break and was in her second year of college. She spoke real proper and looked at me funny when I picked up the wrong fork to eat my salad.

I was out of practice, but I knew I would get back into the swing of things.

I shot her back a look as I saw that she had gotten some spinach caught between her front teeth. I wasn't going to let her be the bit wiser.

After dinner I went back to the guest room and just relaxed on the queen-sized bed.

The mattress was so soft, and I knew I would get a good night's sleep because I didn't have to worry about Mr. Saks waking me up every two to three hours.

I was dozing off into *la-la land* when I heard a knock on the door.

In a groggy voice, I answered, "Who is it?"

"It's me, Earl. Come open the door."

I opened the door and saw that Earl was dressed to the tee.

"Where are you going?"

"Keep your voice down, man. We are going to a party my friend is having. Do you want to come or not?"

"Yeah, but I don't have anything fresh to wear. My mother practically threw me out."

"I got you. Don't worry. We are about the same size, and I have clothes I don't even wear anymore."

I went into his closet and picked out a pair of crisp black jeans with a dragon embroidered on the back pockets, a white tee-shirt with a white zipped up hoodie with rhinestones on it, and a pair of white patent leather sneakers to match.

The funny thing about this was that everything was brand new. I enjoyed popping off the tags.

Earl gave me his white hat to match with a diamond encrusted watch with a white band. When I looked in the mirror, I felt good about myself. I was the definition of fresh to death.

We walked for about ten minutes and went through the back entrance into this house that was twice the size of Uncle Paul's.

The living room was completely white. White leather couches, white carpet, lamps, tables, piano...I had to take off my shoes before I walked on the carpet. Whoever owned the house really had taste.

We quickly went downstairs, and there were about one hundred kids down there. Doing what teenagers do. Earl introduced me to a couple of girls who went to his school and I tried sounding as mature as possible as they asked me questions.

They thought I was a junior in high school, and I wasn't going to correct them. I was having a blast, and I noticed that some people were drinking alcohol.

One of Earl's friends offered me some, but I told him no. They looked at me weird, so I told them I had to drive home.

That kept them off my back. I wasn't going to get caught up with any of that stuff and end up like my father.

Earl looked liked he was about to cave in to the peer pressure, but backed off when I shot him a look that said if he even took a baby sip I'd be telling on him.

The music was bumping, and I danced with a couple of seniors. They were good looking, but they seemed more interested in looking cute.

I heard one girl tell her girlfriend, "This top cost $1,000, and I don't want it smelling like sweat."

After a couple more songs, I sat down for awhile because I was kind of bored.

I didn't know where Earl had disappeared to, so I began looking for him.

I found him talking with some of his friends near the refrigerator.

I stood there trying to seem interested as they talked about what colleges they got accepted to.

I went to the bathroom, but before I entered I heard someone throwing up inside.

I could smell it through the door and went back down to where the music was playing and sat on the couch.

Earl came and found me, pulled me up, and tried convincing me to follow him to see this girl that just walked in.

"Yo, cous, this girl is the finest girl I've ever seen. Wish me luck. I am going to ask her to dance."

"Do your thing. I'll be over here on the couch."

"Alright, suit yourself. Later."

The DJ put on an old disco song [probably from the seventies], and I heard a crowd of kids chanting, *"Ooh, ooh. Go Earl, go Earl, go Earl."*

What was going on? I knew my cousin had two left feet, and I wanted to see what all the fuss was about.

I made my way through the maze of people that had formed a circle and saw Earl dancing like a maniac.

Earl was dancing with a girl who had her back turned to me.

As I came closer, the girl backed up into me. When she turned around, I stood still.

"Roxanne. What are you doing here?"

"The question is, what are you doing here? I am dancing here. I'll speak with you later."

I went over to the couch and began wondering, *How did Roxanne get here?*

Twenty minutes later, Earl came over and said, "Booyah. I got the digits. I am a certified player from the Himalayas."

I laughed. "Yeah, Earl. You are a real Macaroni Toni. Sike."

"Don't hate. Participate and congratulate."

Earl had danced up a storm; after sitting with me on the couch for about twenty minutes, he was sleeping like a baby.

I got up and began looking all around for Roxanne.

I found her talking to one of Earl's friends, and Roxanne told the guy he could call her next week.

That was the second time she had given out her number for the night.

I went up to her as the guy walked away.

"Did you know you were dancing with my cousin?"

"Well, I hope you can dance better than he can. He swore he was killing it. Anyway, I didn't come here to stand around. Let's dance."

Roxanne grabbed me by the hand, and Cupid must have had me on his list because a slow jam came on.

Roxanne moved me close to her, and rested her head on my chest.

Cupid's spell lasted for about ten seconds because a boy who appeared drunk hit the turntable and the record skipped. The DJ changed the music and that's when Roxanne picked up her head, crossed her arms, and began frowning. She stood there for about ten seconds looking around.

"I'll be right back. I'm going to the ladies room to freshen up."

I sat there thinking that too much alcohol messes up everything.

Roxanne came back twenty minutes later.

"Sorry I took so long. I have to go, my ride is leaving. I'll see you in school when your suspension is over."

That is when I realized I really messed up. I wouldn't be able to see Roxanne's pretty face for a whole month.

Earl and I got back to the house around 5:30 in the morning, and it seemed like I just put my head down on my pillow as I heard the sound of the alarm clock.

When I jumped up, I saw it was 6:30 a.m. It took me another ten minutes to turn off that awful sound.

My head was pounding from all the loud music I was around last night. I went to Earl's room, but he wasn't in there.

I looked around a little and saw that he had the VGA2 and practically every game that was out for the system.

As I picked up his controller, Earl came through the door. "What's up, cous? Checking out my VGA2?"

"I didn't know you had all these games. I love this system."

"Dad got that for me last week. I don't have much time to play it, though. I spend most of my time hitting the books."

"So that means you don't mind if I play it while you are at school."

"Knock yourself out. I will be home late; I am taking my SAT prep course tonight. I got a 2,000 last time, but I think I can improve. I am going for a perfect score. Check this quote I heard: 'Good, better, best—never let it rest—until the good becomes better and better becomes the best.'"

"Have fun," I said as I turned on his forty-two-inch plasma TV and his VGA2.

"Later. And by the way, make sure you don't have your crusty feet on my pillows. Matter of fact, put some socks on. Your toes look like fingers."

"Ha, ha, ha, very funny," I said as I threw a pillow at him. After searching through his catalogue of games, I stopped at one in particular and couldn't keep my mouth closed.

Earl had *Tai Chi Reign*.

It was still in its wrapper and it was attached to a plastic bag. I ripped open the plastic bag, and inside I found a golden Tai Chi t-shirt signed by the maker of the game.

I put it on, opened the sealed video game, and put it into the system.

The introduction had this old man sitting with his eyes closed in a forest. Ninjas in different colored suits were in the background sneaking up to attack him.

The graphics were eye-popping, and I could tell that the old man was the master in the game.

Most fighting games were the same, so I pressed the start button to skip the introduction. I picked the practice mode and learned how to execute some basic moves. Then I went back to the start menu and decided to get into some action.

I had four people to choose from: Splitter was a white guy with a Mohawk and scars on his face and wearing a karate gee; Showtime was a black guy with a red bandana around his afro, rocking a tank top and Chinese slippers; Spottie was a hyena that stood up on its hind legs like it was a human; 5679 was a robot that was extremely tall, and its head was shaped like a pineapple.

The crazy thing was that their twelve different boxes that had exclamation marks inside them, but no characters I could choose from. That meant that when I finished the game with all these separate competitors, I would get them.

I went back to the practice mode and began working on a basic kick-kick-punch combo that popped up on the screen when I clicked on the pop-up menu. It took off sixty percent of my opponent's damage, and I practiced that move for about twenty minutes.

I practiced every move that I saw on the pop-up menu. An hour and a half later, I was ready to start playing for real [not beating up on these practice dummies that didn't fight back, which was getting stale].

Each round you had to defeat your opponent three different times before you could move on. There were twelve different opponents you had to defeat before you could reach the Tai Chi Lord. I got to the last board fairly quickly, but it took me twenty times to defeat him.

He was one tough old man.

I was exhausted, so I went downstairs to the refrigerator.

As I walked by the living room, I saw Ms. Clara watching TV and at the same time ordering something on the phone.

That reminded me what Uncle Paul asked me to do.

I ran back upstairs, saved my progress, changed my t-shirt, and went to the basement. I could hardly find space to maneuver.

There were seven different rooms down there, and most of them were filled with Ms. Clara's stuff. I started with room number one. I arranged everything and put the things that were broken in a large plastic bag. I went to room number two and did the same thing.

When I checked my watch, I saw it was 4:30.

I had been down there six hours.

I went back upstairs, jumped in the shower, and afterwards relaxed on my bed.

There was a knock on the door.

"Come in."

Earl strolled in with his book bag on his shoulder.

"What's up, cousin?" I said.

"I see you found *Tai Chi Reign*. Dad got it from one of his patients that just came back from Japan."

"That game is off the hook. I am pretty good at it already."

"So come to my room, and let's get it on."

"Bet. Best out of three."

I loaded the game and picked Showtime and finished off Earl in five minutes flat.

"That's three perfects in a row," I said with a smile on my face.

Earl was not satisfied. He told me it was beginner's luck and loaded the game again. He was tapping the buttons like his life depended on it, but the results were still the same.

"That's three more perfects," I said in a cocky tone. "You want to try again? I'll play you blindfolded."

"Very funny. I give up. You are way too good at this."

As Earl sat at his computer doing some research for a paper, I played for another two hours before Ms. Clara called us for dinner.

My uncle wasn't home from work, and Fredricka was hanging out with some friends.

Ms. Clara was a great cook. I went back for three more helpings of her mouth watering tuna casserole. Ms. Clara made it a point to tell me that she learned everything that has to do with food from watching her favorite cooking show *Cook Like a Top Chef* everyday.

After eating three slices of her homemade cherry pie, I went back to Earl's room and played for another three hours before getting kicked out by Earl who wanted to go to sleep.

Earl let me take the VGA2 to my room, and I played until 12:30 in the morning. I would have played longer, but I turned off the system when I heard footsteps coming upstairs that sounded like Fredricka's.

I wasn't tired and just stared out the window at the stars that seemed so close that I could touch them. It was such a clear night, and I wondered if life could get any better. I knew this lifestyle wouldn't last forever, but I was sure enjoying it.

Three weeks later

I had gotten so good at *Tai Chi Reign* that I had been beating all of Earl's friends on a regular basis. I would bet them a dollar a game, and I would have no less than $500 cash per week.

I didn't save any of that money. I spent it, mostly on being fresh to death.

I bought my first pair of $150 sneakers. They were orange and red patent leather with the laces to match. I didn't even take them out of the box. I was going to wear them the first day back to school. I also bought jeans, hats, belts, and jackets. I had close to a month's worth of outfits without repeating the same thing. That was definitely a step up. Before, I didn't have enough clothes to go three days without trying to mix and match something. I was definitely a Freshboy.

As I sat in the back seat of Uncle Paul's car on the way back home, I felt sad. I wanted to stay with Uncle Paul forever. I was really going to miss his house and all its amenities.

Uncle Paul began thanking me for cleaning up the basement and the garage. I surely wasn't going to miss that part of my stay. I didn't want to ever have to do a task like that again. It took me almost a month to do it.

I shifted my thoughts to Roxanne [a.k.a. Foxy Roxy]. As I closed my eyes, I started smiling as I envisioned seeing her in homeroom and what she would think of me when I showed up with all these new clothes.

The forty-five-minute ride home zoomed by, and I wasn't happy to be back home.

My mother gave me a look that said that she was not going to tolerate any more foolishness.

I waited until we finished dinner before I gave out my surprises. I gave each of my siblings a new outfit from head to toe. My mother didn't pay attention as they hugged me and began trying on their new stuff. Mama was concentrating on the dishes that were piled in the sink.

As Mama made her way to the bathroom, I noticed that she was still hobbling around.

I wished she wouldn't work so much, but I didn't want to tell her that Uncle Paul said that she had arthritis in her knee and it would act up from time to time. Standing on her feet all those hours was only going to worsen her condition. Mama couldn't quit now. How else would we survive?

When she finished washing up, I handed her a beautifully decorated box.

Mama smiled as she tried on her custom shoes.

She gave me a long hug, and I told her to take it easy.

I lied and told her that the shoes were on sale because she began questioning me about the price. I'd do it again in a heartbeat! That was $400 well spent. I haven't seen her smile like that in years.

I also left out the part about me winning the money. My mother would have told me to give it back because I was "doing the devil's work" or what everyone else called gambling.

As soon as I stepped into homeroom everyone was staring at me, including Roxanne. She came right up to me and gave me a big hug. "I've missed you. Look at you. You are looking good!"

I began blushing, and that close encounter carried me through the day.

I was on cloud nine and everything was going good...until I saw Max at lunchtime.

Max made a beeline towards me. Soon as he approached with his boys, I prepared myself to get pounded on.

Max growled, "Our beef is done with. Someone put in a call for you. Personally, I would like to rearrange your frame, but obviously you have friends in high places."

I wasn't quite sure who he was talking about, but I was happy that the only thing on today's menu was fricasseed beef and string beans.

That was the fastest school day that I could remember. Before I knew it, I was back in our apartment.

I told Marcus to watch everyone while I went over to Peter's house to play *Tai Chi Reign*. Earl was nice enough to give it to me because he didn't have time to really play. I think it was because he was terrible at that game.

When I got outside the building, I saw Fred approaching. "Hey, what's up? Long time no see."

"I had to get away from things for a minute. You know. To clear my head."

"I took care of that problem for you."

"What problem?"

"Max and his boys."

"So it was you who put in the OG call."

"I had to. Word on the street was they were going to hurt your mother."

I stood paralyzed and wanted to definitely get out of the neighborhood even quicker. I didn't know what I would do if anyone hurt my family. Especially Mama.

I gave Fred a pound and said, "I really appreciate that. I owe you big. How can I repay you?"

"Don't sweat it. I'll think of something some day," Fred answered with a smile. "I got some business to take care of. I'll see you around."

I went to Peter's apartment and found his father on the couch again, passed out. I whispered to Peter, "He is like a statue. Does he move?"

Peter went over to his father and gently tried to take the TV controller out of his hand. His father started mumbling something I couldn't quite make out and held on to the controller like he was holding on to a cliff for dear life.

We both began snickering softly.

Peter said, "A nuclear explosion couldn't get him up when he falls asleep. But if you try to remove that TV controller, he is liable to take your head off. Don't ever mess with his remote control."

We went to Peter's room, and we began playing *Tai Chi Reign*. Beating Peter wasn't much fun.

To test my skills, I put it on the hardest setting, and I was still able to beat the game like it was on easy.

As I continued playing, Peter sat at his desk surfing the Internet. "Yo. Just. Check this out."

"Wait a minute, I am on the last stage."

"Nah. Check it out now."

I put the game on pause and read what was on the VGA2 website: "*To all* Tai Chi Reign *players. On the date we will later disclose, there will be a* Tai Chi Reign *tournament. You will be battling it out for the grand prize of three million dollars. There is only one winner, and second and third place don't count. To be an eligible contestant, you have to beat the game on the hard setting with eight different characters in under an hour's time. To get the code to enter, please click the link below. You have three weeks to submit your entries.*"

I clicked on the website, entered all the required information, and decided that I would need to master eight different characters before I'd be ready.

I went on another website that charged a dollar per page to access any characters moves for *Tai Chi Reign*.

I needed eighty pages for the eight characters I picked.

I pulled out the money Earl had lent me the day I left and handed it to Peter. Peter used his mother's credit card that he was only use when there was an emergency and we downloaded the moves and printed the pages.

After playing a couple more games against the computer, I went home.

Nothing had really changed from when I left. Marcus's head was still buried in the books, Albert was still playing with his toys, and Alicia was still getting on my nerves.

"Well, brother. It has been real quiet since you haven't been around," Alicia said with a smile. "I hope you are going to behave yourself, because next time Mama said she will be sending you to Japan to live with Daddy."

I couldn't see myself living with my father and just ignored her and began watching TV.

I went to my room and grabbed some index cards I had under the bed. I began copying the moves for all the separate players and decided that I would try to memorize them for a week before playing *Tai Chi Reign* again.

Later on that night, as I sat staring at the ceiling, I thought about what I could do with the money. I could buy us a new home. I could pay off my mother's credit card debts. I could buy new clothes for everyone. I could impress Roxanne and make her my girl, and maybe just maybe my father would come back home and we could be a family again.

This money would automatically solve all our problems.

For the rest of the week I was physically at school, but if you were to look in my notebook you wouldn't see any notes.

I would make-believe I was writing notes, but in the meantime I was memorizing the moves that I had taped on the inside of my notebook. I did this during the first four periods of my school day. I focused my attention to the ten to fifteen string combinations because that would help me beat my opponents more effectively.

And during the last four periods of the day, I'd make-believe that I had a controller in my hands, tapping buttons, and making sound effects.

Max had caught me doing this in gym class and yelled, "I told you this guy is a weirdo. Look at him talking to himself. Hey, Justin. What is your invisible friend's name?"

Studying these moves occupied every moment of my school day, and there were many times I didn't eat lunch.

My grades were suffering. I received a 40 on my math test, 30 on my English test, and 25 on my history test.

I was going to be failing all my classes for the second marking period in a row, but I kept telling myself that if I mastered these moves and won this money then I wouldn't have to worry about school at all.

I had it all thought out.

I could win the money before the marking period was over. And even though my mother would be upset about my grades I would inform her that we were officially rich.

Now that would be a happy ending.

One week later

I was sitting on the couch when the phone rang. I didn't want to pick it up, but Alicia was working on her homework, and I didn't want to argue with her.

I recognized the operator's voice and knew that it had to be a collect call from my father.

"Yeah, I'll accept the charges."

"Hello. Who am I speaking to?" my father asked.

"Justin. What's up?"

"Well, you know. Just trying to work some things out. Hoping to get back home soon."

"Yeah, right. You sound like the superintendent in this crummy building. Maybe you guys are brothers," I mumbled under my breath.

"Speak up, son. I can't hear you."

"Nothing, Dad. That sounds great. I am going to let you speak to Marcus."

As I listened, Marcus was telling my father about his high school and college plans. I wanted to start singing, *"Kumbaya my lord, Kumbaya. Oh, Lord, Kumbaya."*

The thought of school made me think about someone deliberately dragging their nails across a blackboard. Annoying!

I wanted to practice even more, so I told everyone I was leaving and went to Peter's house.

I hadn't physically touched a controller in a week and opted to try out my new moves during practice mode.

It felt great being able to execute five to ten string combinations with such ease. I knew every move possible for eight different characters, and I wanted to see what I could do against competition. The cool thing about the VGA2 was that you could play people via the Internet, so I typed in the address to a website that I heard all the top *Tai Chi Reign* players went on.

I was playing this guy from Spain who after blocking for ten minutes straight I was declared the winner. Next was a guy from Germany who I beat in two minutes.

I heard they both hadn't lost a game since *Tai Chi Reign* came out.

It was official in my mind. I was a runaway train that couldn't be stopped.

I went back to Peter's computer and got the entry code, punched it in my VGA2, and sat ready to qualify for the tournament.

Across the screen read in big block letters.

HELLO CONTESTANTS:
YOU HAVE SIX TRIES TO COMPLETE THE TASK OF BEATING TAI CHI REIGN *WITH EIGHT CHARACTERS IN UNDER AN HOUR. IF YOU DON'T QUALIFY, YOU CANNOT TRY AGAIN. YOUR CODE WILL NOT WORK. GOOD LUCK!!!!!!!!!*

I had on the *Tai Chi Reign* shirt Earl gave me and was ready to get things poppin'.

After the game was fully loaded and I got to the main screen, I noticed that all the graphics were totally upgraded.

As I began the first fight, I recognized that the computer countered every move I tried.

It was absolutely frustrating. I threw the controller down and almost broke it after losing in the first round.

Peter looked on in amazement. He went on the Internet and found out from a chat room that the maker of the game was the one who designed the challenge; he had all the opponents mirror the challengers' moves to make it extremely hard to win. You had to really know how to mask your moves and switch them up before you did them.

I turned off the system in disgust and went back home.

Two weeks later

The video game fairies must have known that I wanted this opportunity badly, because on my sixth time I beat the game.

I quickly saved the game on the memory card and screamed at the top of my lungs while embracing Peter.

I didn't think it was possible, but on my way out I saw Peter's father on his hands and knees looking around for the TV controller. He was so preoccupied searching for the controller that he didn't even pay me any mind as I shut the door.

When I got inside my apartment, I called Earl and called in another favor. I told him that I would make it up to him when I won the money.

Thirty minutes later we were enjoying food from Russiani's.

Alicia and Marcus wanted to know what we were celebrating, but I didn't let the cat out of the bag.

I left mother's favorite, shrimp scampi, with a note on it telling her that Earl sent this and that I loved her.

After third period, I cut class and went straight to the Post Office. I mailed off the memory card and decided that I didn't want to go back to school, so I went back home.

Before I could get the key in the door, I saw Mr. Saks.

He didn't have to say a word. I knew that I was busted. After a brief stare down [like a bull watching the matador], Mr. Saks asked me if I could help him with some stuff in his apartment.

"I'm busy."

But after he explained that he would tell my mother that I cut school, I realized that wasn't a bad idea after all.

When we got inside his apartment, I realized that Mr. Saks was not only old, he was also a slob. He had pizza boxes scattered all over the place that reminded me of abstract art.

He also had big—I mean mutant-type big—roaches running up and down the apartment like they were training for the Olympics.

His sink was full of dishes that were forming mold, and he had so much dust on the floor it looked like gray carpeting.

"Justin, have a seat."

I looked at the couch that he must have purchased in the early 1950s and said, "I'm cool. I'd rather stand if you don't mind."

"Not at all."

I dodged a bullet. If I would have sat on that couch I would have needed a *triple cooties shot.*

I didn't see one TV in the whole apartment, and I wondered what he did to entertain himself. I let curiosity get the best of me.

"Mr. Saks, what do you do to entertain yourself?"

He had an answer filled with a lot of information.

"Do you know that the average American watches about four hours of TV a day. That is a total of twenty-eight hours a week. Meaning, by the end of the year you'd be watching two months of non-stop TV. By the time you turn around sixty-five, you would've spent nine years of your life watching TV."

I tried to seem interested as he rambled off some other facts, but I was wondering how long I would have to stay in there, practically listening and holding my breath at the same time.

Mr. Saks' apartment smelled like doggie doo-doo mixed with a cup of urine, feet casserole, and topped off with 200 farts. Rancid was the word Alicia would have used.

Mr. Saks finally stopped talking and I followed him to what would have been my mother's room.

As soon as he opened the door, I smelled the scent of fresh roses and noticed that this room was surprisingly spotless. The floor was so polished that I could see my own reflection on the wood.

It was like having an oasis in the middle of the desert.

Mr. Saks had these beautiful mahogany bookcases with hundred of books neatly arranged on them. The bookcases were standing against the three sides of the room, and the only empty space was the window that had these exotic looking plants perched on the sill.

Near the window lay a black leather couch accompanied by a La-Z-Boy chair that had an antique looking nightstand next to it.

The ceiling had about thirty different light fixtures. Mr. Saks drew the curtains and turned on the lights and the whole room lit up like a Christmas tree.

"These are my prized possessions. I have a lot of different kinds of books, but my favorite topic is philosophy. You do know what that means, right?"

I hoped this wasn't a pop quiz and answered, "Of course I do."

Mr. Saks cracked open a book and read out loud, *"Each man or woman governs their life by a philosophy. The philosophy he or she subscribes to is their worldview. It is designed by one's perception or how one perceives the world around us. Constantly taking in information, synthesizing it, and coming up with conclusions. But one must be careful not to take everything in at once and reach conclusions that are not true, or that are half truths, and deem them as valid conclusions."*

Mr. Saks was obviously speaking another language. I wished he would go back to speaking English.

After twenty minutes of non-stop rambling, he closed the book and said, "In summation. Knowledge is priceless, Justin."

Mr. Saks looked at me like he was waiting for a response. I could only think of what Marcus loved to say. "Knowledge is power."

I left his apartment shortly after he tried to offer me something to drink. Mr. Saks promised he wouldn't tell as long as he didn't see me cutting school again. I tuned out the "school is important" message because I didn't want to hear that again.

When school was let out for dismissal, I was in front of the school acting as if I was there all day. I walked with my siblings and Peter home.

I didn't go upstairs with them but went straight to Peter's house and popped in *Tai Chi Reign*.

I hooked it up with the Internet link and was whooping another boy from China who was supposed to be the best player in his province.

It became late, so I went home and went straight to bed.

I managed to roll out of bed the next morning thinking about Roxanne.

Roxanne had been real nice to me since I had all these fresh outfits. Actually, my stock had risen tremendously.

I had male and female groupies, and everyone wanted to sit near me and be my friend. I loved the way this felt; for once, I knew that everyone else knew that I existed.

I was no longer in the shadow of Marcus, who everyone knew because of his academic work. The teachers were the only people who weren't really impressed. Who cared, though? I didn't want them to be my friends, anyway.

The day went by quickly, and I actually stayed in school all day because people were treating me like I a superstar. That was my definition of a fun filled school day.

I went back to Peter's house and played *Tai Chi Reign*. I had a lot of time on my hands because my mother had been working even later the last couple of days.

After a couple of hours of disposing of some kids from Australia, I headed home.

As I began putting my key in the door, I noticed it was slightly ajar. I entered cautiously and saw my mother sitting on the couch with her arms crossed and a large black plastic bag sitting near her feet.

"Hi, Mama. You're home early."

"Yes, I am. How is school?"

"School is fine," I answered confidently, trying to be as cool as I could be.

"I see. I see."

"Where is everyone?"

"Everyone is asleep. Do you know what time it is? It is already 8 o'clock, that's what time it is," she answered, not really giving me an opportunity to answer. "Where have you been?"

"I was at a classmate's house doing some homework. We have this project that is really important to our grades."

"Really. Let me see what you got so far."

"My classmate has all the notes, Mama. I'll let you see it tomorrow."

My mother got up off the couch, came close to me, and strained her neck upwards.

"You must take me for a fool," she said in disgust. "The school called my job today and informed me of your cutting, lateness, and atrocious grades again."

Mama started pacing up and down our apartment.

"I am going to be sending you to your father in two months, so enjoy the rest of your time here."

I closed my eyes, hoping that she was just pulling my leg.

"But, Mama. You can't. I don't want to move."

"I don't know what you want to do. But I will not have you living here, not abiding by my rules. You are setting a bad example for your siblings. Don't you care? All you seem to care about is looking fly these days and getting what 'guap.' You must really think I am an idiot. It was Earl who got you all those clothes. I called him, and he told me that you have been gambling. Gambling. How could you?"

"Mama, I didn't lose. Not once. It was a sure bet."

"I don't care. That is not a good habit to start," she said, trying to keep her voice down. "Well, you know what? You like to lie, and you think money is everything."

"No, Mama. It's not like that at all."

"Well, not in here. I don't want anything in here that was won gambling."

My mother threw the plastic bag at me. When I looked inside, I saw all my new clothes cut into small pieces, even my sneakers. Everything looked like they were put through a shredder.

"You will wear what I provide for you and appreciate that. If not, you can go naked. Do you hear me? So many people don't have anything at all. I may not provide the latest, but I do what I can afford."

I was steaming mad and shot back at my mother, "Look who is talking. Remember all those expensive clothes you used to have. All that jewelry. All those nice things. Dad messed all those things up. Dad did. You could have stopped him if you weren't so involved in being fly yourself. I want that lifestyle again, Mama, and I am going to get it. Watch! I am going to get it, and no one can stop me."

My mother didn't respond. She turned her back to me, went straight to her room, and slammed the door.

Even though it was hard staying in school all day, I did so for the next week straight. No cutting. No lateness.

I started making more of an effort and managed to get 65's on my next couple of tests.

As my clothes went, so did my newfound stardom. Roxanne went back to just barely waving and I was back to eating lunch with only Peter.

My mother had been working extra hours because the credit card bill collectors had been calling; some of her accounts even went into collection.

I had to resume bribing Alicia because I was going to Peter's house to play *Tai Chi Reign*.

I wasn't able to concentrate after having that conversation with my mother and was so down in the dumps that I couldn't even beat Peter.

I gave up after losing another five times in a row as Peter kept using the same kick-kick-punch-punch combo. Peter enjoyed beating me and tried to convince me to stay and play again.

I left his apartment and headed home. As soon as I got in, I went straight to my top bunk and noticed there was an enveloped addressed to me on my pillow.

I went back in the living room and asked who it was from.

Alicia responded, "I don't know, smartie pants. You have to open it and see. The express guy just dropped it off, and I signed for it."

I opened the package and inside was a gold envelope with a VGA2 seal on it.

I opened the envelope and read its contents aloud:

Dear Mr. Justin Stanford,

Congratulations on getting past the first phase of the contest. You are one of the 160 lucky contestants who will get to compete for a grand prize of $3 million. Don't get too excited, because you will have to win quite a few games before you get to compete for the money. You will get a chance to beat one of your peers, and, as a bonus you'll be able to play a few games with the creator of the game and be a character in Tai Chi Reign 2 *coming out next year.*

P.S. Look in the package and see two round trip tickets to sunny Montego Bay, Jamaica. You have twenty-four hours to confirm your receipt of this package.

I started jumping up and down. Marcus, who was reading the letter over my shoulder, was in shock.

"I didn't know you entered that contest."

"Yup. I'm pretty good, too," I said, still jumping up and down like a three-year-old.

Alicia jumped in, "I guess that is why you were spending all that time with Peter, huh. I bet you been playing over there.

Where did you guys get that system, anyway? Who stole it? Because I know both you guys are B R O K E."

"Shut up, Alicia. You are so nosey. You are always in someone's business."

"I wouldn't say nosey, brother. I would say inquisitive. Look it up."

"Soon you will be begging me for money. Then I will remember all these wisecracks."

Albert sat playing with his Teenage Mutant Ninja Turtles toys and said, "Cowabunga dude. Cowabunga."

I was excited and called Peter to tell him the good news. He reminded me that, if I won the money, he should get some because he had been helping me practice and all.

I laughed and told him he would be on my list.

I went to the refrigerator and poured myself the biggest glass of Kool-Aid I could and practiced in a Jamaican accent that I had heard on TV.

"No problem, man. Everyt'ing irie."

I didn't know what "irie" meant, but it sure sounded cool.

Marcus began laughing, and we started dancing around like we were listening to reggae music.

I liked reggae music, especially the dance hall reggae music. It seemed like every song came with its own dance.

As we continued dancing in the living room, Alicia interrupted us with her annoying voice.

"I don't think you'll be going to Jamaica," she said with a devilish grin on her face.

"What are you talking about?" I replied.

"You are such a bozo. Did you read the fine print on the bottom of the page?"

"What fine print?"

Alicia put the paper close to my face then snatched it back, ran into Mama's room, and locked the door.

I had my ear against the door, and I heard her giggling and reading even louder behind the door.

Alicia said, imitating a man's voice, "All contestants under the age of eighteen must be accompanied by a parent."

Alicia then pushed the letter under the door. I quickly read it and became quiet. She was right.

Alicia heard my silence and came out of the room and said, "You know Mama isn't going to go with you. Because to her this is gambling, and she doesn't want any part of anything that sounds like gambling."

I stood still and plopped myself down on the couch.

I felt sick, and Marcus became quiet as well.

We both knew Alicia was right. There was no way that Mama was going to let me go.

Mama walked through the door around midnight. I took her coat and put the kettle on to boil some water to put in a basin so she could soak her feet.

As she sat on the couch, I already had her favorite meal, lasagna, warming in our little oven.

"Where did you get that?"

"I made it myself. Just sit down. I will give you a neck massage."

Mama complied with my wishes, and I was massaging her neck as she sat down soaking her feet.

"I was thinking, Mama. What would you do if we had a lot of money? Would you move out?"

"Of course, baby. But I am comfortable where I am for the time being. This place is better than what some people have. I have to be grateful."

It was time to lead her down the path I wanted.

"Well, Mama I think I can get $3 million."

"Baby, stop dreaming. I don't want to hear any foolishness tonight. I had a long day."

"For real, Mama," I answered as I handed her the gold envelope.

"What's this?" She said as she asked me to get her reading glasses.

"You'll see, Mama."

Mama took her time reading the letter then handed it back to me, got up, and headed to the bathroom.

"But, Mama. Can I go?" I pleaded. "This is an opportunity of a lifetime. This is what we all need. I know I can win."

"I can't afford to take off any time."

"Mama, you have some personal days that you haven't used yet. You could if you want."

"No! I am not going. That is gambling. Ask your father when he calls; maybe he can go with you."

"Mama, we haven't seen Dad in years, and it is not like you can call him. Plus, I have to confirm my entry in twenty-four hours."

"Justin, I don't want to repeat myself. I am tired, and you are working my nerves. Please don't get me started. I am not going to ask you when you have been playing this game and how you got so good to even qualify. Is this why your grades are suffering? I am not going to get upset anymore. You better hope for a miracle because I am not going. Ask your father when he calls."

My mother went inside the bathroom and shut the door.

I realized the conversation was completely over.

My opportunity was slipping away, and I was furious. This was the second time that I really wanted something to happen, and this was the result. I was batting zero for two.

I went to my room and made my way to the top bunk.

My brother was still awake. I told him what happened, and he gave me some advice, "Why don't you visualize Dad calling tomorrow?"

"What are the chances that will happen?"

"I don't know, but give it a try."

I thought Marcus was going to tell me to give up and move on and give me the long drawn out education spiel. But he was right. I really had no alternatives. I sat and meditated silently; it wasn't long, but I got straight to the point.

"If anyone out in the Universe is listening, give me this opportunity, and I will forever be thankful."

I must have been sleeping like a rock because I didn't wake up until I heard a loud shriek coming from the living room. When I got to the living room, Alicia was screaming, "Someone smash that ugly roach."

I wanted the roach to somehow mysteriously attack Alicia, maybe just crawl up her arm or, even better, her face. After a short chase, I smashed the roach to smithereens with her favorite sneakers.

"Eee, that is nasty. Justin, can you clean that stuff off my sneaker. I don't want to go anywhere near it."

This was my opportunity to get back at her. "Of course I can, sis. But that will be twenty dollars."

"I am not paying you anything. I'll ask Marcus."

Marcus looked at Alicia and said, "I hate roaches, too. I am not going near your sneaker. Not even for a hundred dollars."

I knew Marcus wasn't that scared of roaches, and he winked at me when Alicia turned her back.

Alicia hurried back in the room, grabbed a twenty-dollar bill out of her piggy bank, gave it to me, and said, "Here, just make sure it is nice and clean."

I snickered. "Your wish is my command. It was nice doing business with you."

I went to the bathroom, showered, got dressed, and went to the kitchen to get some milk for my cereal. I looked at the clock and realized I had twenty minutes left before we had to go to school. I ate my cereal then came to the realization that my father wasn't going to call.

I grabbed my stuff, headed out the door, and quickly made an about face because I had forgotten my lunch money in my other pants.

When I was on my way out, I looked on the floor next to my brother's Teenage Mutant Ninja Turtle toy and saw the telephone receiver lying behind it.

The phone was off the hook.

It had to be Alicia when she was running all over the place when she saw a roach.

I ran back outside, quickly caught up to my siblings, and told them to go ahead because I had left my homework.

Alicia gave me a funny look and said, "Yeah right."

I ignored her and quickly went back to our apartment.

I figured the phone had been off for at least forty minutes, and I had about seventeen minutes to wait in the apartment before I would be officially late for school. Which was really pushing it, because I would have to haul some serious tail.

I sat next to the receiver, hoping that somehow the phone would start ringing. Eight minutes later, the phone did ring.

The operator said, "I have a collect call from—"

I interrupted the operator in mid-sentence. "I accept. I accept. Hello, Dad."

"Hello, Pedro," a man answered in a deep Spanish accent.

I was disappointed.

"Nobody named Pedro lives here."

"You sure this isn't Pedro."

I was wasting time. After I repeated my phone number to him five times in a row, he said, "Sorry about that. I always mix up the sixes and the nines."

He sounded like he wanted to talk, so I hung up the phone as he blabbed about how it was hot in Puerto Rico and how was the weather in New York.

I looked at the clock again. I only had seven minutes.

The phone rang again, but it wasn't my father. It was a bill collector. They were going on about how an outstanding bill was affecting my mother's credit score, and I replied, "You will have to speak to her about that. I don't pay any bills in here."

I only had five minutes to get to school. If the phone didn't ring in about sixty seconds, there was no way I was going to make it.

The phone rang, and the operator said, "I have a collect call from Phillip Stanford. Will you accept the charges?"

I yelled "yes" so loudly the operator asked if I was on medication.

"Hello, Dad. How is everything going?" I said in an excited voice.

"Is this Justin?"

"Of course, Dad. Your first born."

"Are you okay, son? You haven't been this nice to me since you were a young boy and you tried to convince me that having a mo-ped was the best Christmas gift and that you didn't need a helmet."

I answered in the calmest, non-argumentative voice I could muster. "Not at all, Dad. I know how much you love me and you are always looking out for me."

"Let's cut to the chase. What do you want?"

I told my father about the contest.

After a minute of dead silence, he said, "I'll meet you in Montego Bay. Let me just tell my boss I have a family emergency."

I hung up the phone, called the VGA2 hotline, and confirmed my entry into the contest.

I was happy; at the same time it dawned on me that my father hadn't been home in years, but as soon as he had the opportunity to make it big, he was all in. I was definitely not trying to get myself too worked up, though. I had to remain as calm as possible. I had five days to practice and get myself ready for an opportunity of a lifetime.

As I sat on the couch saying my goodbyes to my family, I realized that I had to win the money. This was our meal ticket out of this neighborhood.

As I began leaving, Alicia made me promise not to read the note that she stuffed into my pocket until I got on the plane.

The cab driver drove like a madman to get me to LaGuardia Airport. After erratically [a word Alicia used to describe my studying habits] weaving in and out of traffic like he was playing dodge ball, we got their unharmed.

As I exited his cab, he asked for a tip.

"I have a tip for you. Don't drive so fast you could kill someone." I responded as I closed his car door.

He started cursing at me and almost ran over my toes as he sped off.

I checked in my one suitcase and after the security check, I waited patiently for the boarding call.

I hadn't been on a plane since I was young, and even that time I didn't remember everything.

Most of the passengers waiting to board were from Jamaica, and this cute Jamaican girl said with her accent, "Hello. How are you doing?"

I answered in my best Jamaican accent, "Everyt'ing irie."

She chuckled and told me that is what most tourists said. She suggested I used "all fruits ripe"—which meant "everything is going well"—would help me to blend in a lot better.

I boarded the plane and sat in my first class seat. First class had better seats, wider leg space, our own bathroom, and stewardesses to attend to our needs.

I looked out the window and got ready for my three-and-a-half-hour flight.

I heard a familiar voice coming down the aisle. I could spot his big blockhead from five miles away. It was Earl's friend Jeremy. He put his bag right on the empty seat next to me.

"Jeremy, what's good? You going on vacation?" I said.

"Nah. Going to win $3 million this weekend."

"For real? At the VGA2 contest?" I said, as Jeremy looked shocked that I knew about the contest. "Well, good luck on trying to win second because first place belongs to me."

Jeremy twisted up his face like he smelled something foul. "Talk is cheap. They don't call me Mr. Fifteen String for nothing."

Jeremy was really good in executing fifteen string combos. Which was practically impossible, especially being able to do it five times in a row.

I started getting nervous until I remembered one important thing: Jeremy did all these complicated moves in practice mode.

It is real easy beating up on a computer in practice made; they are designed not to fight back. *Let's see what you do when you are on the defensive. You'll probably fold like a lawn chair.*

I closed my eyes during the flight and tried getting some rest. I was jolted out of my sleep when Jeremy's snoring got out of control. I went into my pocket and took out Alicia's note.

Good luck, brother. I know you can do it. I believe in you, and even though I don't say it often, you are the best brother a person could have. Love, Alicia.

I smiled. Alicia could be such a sweetheart sometimes, but she probably was trying to load her bases just in case I did win. She was no dummy and didn't want to be left out of anything.

I nudged Jeremy; after I did it four more times, he finally stopped snoring.

I couldn't get back to sleep, so I took out my notebook and started memorizing my moves.

When I finally closed my eyes, I heard the stewardess telling us to fasten our seatbelts because we were landing.

It was a smooth landing. When we got through Customs, I began looking for my father. I was waiting so long that I figured this was typical Dad and he was bailing on me. I knew he couldn't be trusted. I called home and told Mama what was going on, and she told me that he had missed his flight and would arrive in Montego Bay in five hours. I gave Mama the address to where I was staying.

As I exited the airport, I felt the Jamaican sun. It wasn't like the humidity I was used to in New York. It was just hot. When I looked around at all the bright colors coming from my surroundings, I realized I was in paradise.

A driver was holding a sign that read "Justin Stanford;" when I walked up to him, he took my bags and we headed to his car. He was driving a small car that had an interesting color scheme: yellow hood, blue doors, orange top, and mismatched hubcaps. He had the nerve to have tinted windows, like anyone really wanted to look inside that car.

When I got inside the back of the car, it smelled like a cow took a dump. I looked around to make sure I didn't sit or step in anything.

What kind of treatment was that? The sponsors must have been trying to cut costs wherever they could.

I don't blame them, I thought. I was going to make them cough up three million dollars.

After a twenty-five-minute ride, we arrived in an upscale neighborhood. All the homes were incredible. I must have had my mouth open because the driver said, in a deep Jamaican accent, "You think we are all poor down here. Some of us are doing big things. You hear? Big things. Hard work pays off in the end."

Donovan [who told me his nickname was beenie, which meant small, which was hilarious because he was far from small] was right.

We passed this one home that rivaled Uncle Paul's. Beenie made sure to tell me that the house had a swimming pool on the roof. It made some of the homes in Selden, New York, look like shacks.

When we got to the house I was staying, I felt honored.

I was greeted by this older Jamaican couple who were pleasant. They actually spoke with clear English accents.

The inside of the house was elegantly decorated. Beautiful wooden floors and the paintings of different Caribbean scenery were breathtaking.

I wondered if they knew Ms. Miles because, as I walked through the house, I checked to see if I could locate any dust. There was none to be found.

They ushered me to my room that had enough space for six people at least. I quickly put away my things and went to the bathroom, where I saw the Jacuzzi.

I didn't want to waste any time and was in the Jacuzzi faster than someone could say "boo." I sat in there for two hours, soaking up every moment of this luxurious experience before getting a quick shower.

I got dressed, went downstairs, and was shown the game room, where I saw a 103-inch HD plasma TV, with the VGA2 system lying in the middle of the room.

I wasted no time and began playing.

Three hours later, I took a break when dinner was announced.

I was told I'd be eating West Indian cuisine: curried goat, ackee and salt fish [which I was told was the national dish], rice and peas, plantain, and green yams.

I had never tasted any of that before, but I was pleasantly surprised.

When I was finished, I was informed that there was someone there to see me.

As I came out, I saw my father.

He looked so different to me. I wouldn't have been able to point him out in the street.

"Come here, son, and give your Dad a hug."

I was still harboring some resentment and gave him a firm handshake instead.

He looked a little disappointed, but I didn't care about his feelings.

My father was shorter than I remembered. He appeared uncomfortable, as we looked at each other eye to eye. His hair was much shorter and gray all over, and he was sporting a silver goatee with connecting sideburns.

"Dad, we have to do something about that gray hair. It makes you look older."

"It's okay, son. I am as old as I am. I been through a lot, and I am trying to get my life back together."

I wanted to say, "What about what your family has been through?" But I told myself I had to focus on the money.

I helped him take his bags to his room. When he saw how beautiful the house looked, he began crying.

He began telling the couple how he used to have a beautiful home, how he lost everything, and that he had never felt any comfort since. They began comforting him, but I didn't want to listen, so I went back in the Jacuzzi to keep my mind relaxed.

All the contestants were ushered into a banquet size room in the fancy Ritz Carlton Hotel. I was ready to do what I came to do. The organizers repeated that only 160 people in the whole world had qualified for the tournament.

It was like the college basketball tournament. There were twenty different brackets where the players were seeded one through eight. Number one got an automatic pass to the second round. I was seeded number one, and so was Earl's friend Jeremy. So many countries were present: Argentina, Italy, China, South Africa, Germany, Canada, and Mexico. Some people didn't speak English, but when the game started, they knew how to use that controller. Some people even talked to the controller, willing it to bring home a win.

It didn't work, because you either had it or you didn't. The organizers were thorough. As soon as you lost, you were to go back to where you were staying, get you stuff, and make your way back to the airport. As they say, "Win or go home."

At the end of the night, all the winners were announced. After numbers two through eight battled to see who was best, they were twenty people left who were the victors in their bracket, plus twenty people who got an automatic pass to the second round. A total of forty people remained.

It was a tiring day, watching people duke it out.

It was completely dark when I left.

When I got back to the Brook's home I went straight to my room and quickly showered.

I came back downstairs when dinner was announced. After I gobbled everything up, I went back upstairs and went straight to sleep. I was exhausted.

I looked on the board [which had on it all the fights for the day] and saw that I was up to play first.

The rules were not hard to understand. If you defeated your opponent three times you moved on to the next round.

I was playing someone who looked old enough to be my father. He had red hair, freckles, and very cross-eyed. I couldn't tell if he was looking at me or looking at the screen. When I sat down in a high chair, he said, "Bonjour," then added in English, "I am going to dispose of you quickly."

I loved when people trash talked. "Well, in a few minutes, I'll be saying 'Adieu'." I laughed because I learned that from Alicia, who is learning French from some tapes Marcus gave her.

Pierre [what a typical French name] snarled at me, and we got straight down to business.

Pierre was in a groove and quickly beat me two times then started gloating.

He was undeniably good, and I took in a deep breath to calm myself down.

After a couple of quick combos, I beat him two times in a row.

Pierre began speaking in French to his controller, but the extent of my French was only hello and goodbye.

It was the last round. As soon as we began, I managed to get out a ten-string combo. Pierre didn't even know what hit him.

I was elated [another word Alicia used when she got her way].

Pierre threw down the controller, as he got out of his chair.

I laughed and said, "Adieu Pierre, Adieu."

Pierre gave me a dirty look and began saying something in French. I figured he was cursing at me because he was wearing anger all over his face.

A couple of hours later, there were only twenty contestants remaining.

The organizers announced that we shouldn't go too far because we would be playing again in about an hour.

As I came out of the room, my father greeted me. "Son, how did you do?"

"A piece of cake."

"You were always cocky with those games. Remember when I bought your first game system for Christmas?"

I didn't answer because that was the last Christmas we spent together and the only good memory I had of my father. I was so mad the day someone broke into our apartment and stole it. It was old, but it had a sentimental value to me.

I was up again and saw Jeremy sitting across from me.

He greeted me, and we got it going.

Jeremy was no match. I finished him off by executing three ten-string combos in a row. They say practice makes perfect, and that's exactly how I beat him: three *perrr-fects* in a row.

Hard work pays off, I thought.

At the end of the night, we were told that we were down to ten contestants and we should all return tomorrow.

My father wanted to talk that night, but I told him I was tired. Truthfully, I was focused on getting that money. After all, that was what I was there for.

My next opponent was from India, and I finished him off as quickly as he sat down.

I had a lot of time on my hands. I watched other players sit down then get up.

There were only five contestants left.

Unbelievably, someone had been winning faster than me. Because their combined time in wins was the lowest in minutes played, they had an automatic pass to the finals.

My next round was challenging, but after a lot of blocking my opponents' moves, I was declared the winner forty-five minutes later.

My fingers were aching. *I must be getting videogamefingeritis*, I thought.

The scheduling was brutal.

I beat my next opponent [Fannie from Wyoming], who was old enough to be my grandmother.

She got so mad when I beat her that she took out her dentures and threw them at the screen as she exited the room.

I was happy when they told me I was going to the finals.

I went to the lobby looking for my father but couldn't find him anywhere.

I searched all over the hotel and decided to check the one place I hoped he wasn't.

Jackpot! I saw my father sitting at the bar, laughing uncontrollably with a glass in his hand.

"You're drunk. How could you?" I said as I grabbed the glass out of his hand.

"Wait a minute, son. I can explain."

"Explain? What is there to explain? I can't believe you."

In a nonchalant manner, he said, "Take a smell of the glass."

"I don't want to smell it. I know what it is."

"Well, suit yourself," he said as he took another sip.

I was boiling mad and grabbed the glass from out of his hand again, put it to my nostrils, and took in a deep draw to prove my point.

I had to take another sniff because I was dead wrong.

It was Club soda, not vodka on the rocks (which my mother told me was his favorite drink).

"Son, I haven't had a drink in five years. I'm not all bad. I told you, I'm working on things. I am just here to support you. Just give me a chance."

For the first time, I could tell he was being sincere.

I sat next to him, and we talked liked he had never been absent from my life.

We were interrupted when the organizer informed me that I had to come back for the finals.

There were cameras everywhere, and I was told it would be broadcasted on TV all over the world, including the United States.

I had my father go back to the Brook's home and get my favorite outfit. It was my playa outfit, and it reminded me of the first time Roxanne came to my apartment. I wanted to look good on TV; maybe Roxanne was watching.

My father came back before we were set to go on air. After getting dressed, I was ready for action.

I looked at my opponent and stood motionless.

It was a girl.

Her nametag said "Precious."

Precious had her hair in pigtails with pink ribbons, and she knew I was thinking this must be a joke.

"What is wrong with your face? You better fix it because you are going to get beaten by a girl. Don't start crying like what you boys love to say, 'like a girl'."

Her confidence shook me; I dropped the controller on the ground, and it broke into four pieces. They quickly handed me another controller. I stared at Precious again and read her bright yellow t-shirt with neon pink lettering. "*There is nothing sweeter than beating a boy.*"

I watched as Precious focused on the screen. She appeared as cool as a cucumber while I wondered if she was really that good.

We were told that it was first one to five wins.

I didn't start off too well, and she seemed to counter every move I did. "I know how you think and what you'll do. No ten-string combos today."

I couldn't get any of my ten-string combos out. I was completely frustrated.

Precious, on the other hand, was handing out fifteen-string combos like it was part of her DNA. Ten short minutes later, she had beaten me four straight times with four straight perfects.

How could someone who could be no older than nine years old be so good?

Beads of sweat raced off my forehead and my silk shirt was totally drenched.

I looked over to my father for support, and he gave me the look that said, "I believe in you, son."

Everyone else had a look that said, "Bring in the coroner because someone is a dead man walking."

For some reason, Peter's playing style popped into my head.

I began using a quick kick-kick-punch-punch combo, and Precious got frustrated after I won four games doing the same combination.

"Stop cheesing. Is that all the moves you have? You are pathetic."

The last game was for all the marbles.

I didn't start off right, as Precious executed a quick ten-string combo [which I couldn't block fast enough] and took off almost all my energy.

Actually, my energy was so low that if I even blocked her next move, it would be over.

I began searching in my head for a move and remembered one move that, if I executed well, would take off all her energy. Precious's character came running at me, and I jumped over her, pinned her down backwards, and executed the finishing move that hit her twenty times.

Precious was screaming out loud when I was declared the winner and began crying uncontrollably.

"Look who is crying like a girl now," I said, sticking out my tongue. "Na Na Na Na!"

Precious looked like she was going to punch me, but her mother gave her a look, and she immediately came over and congratulated me.

My father came running into the room screaming, "That's my son. I knew you could do it. That's what I'm talking about. "

The moment didn't really register until I received the three million dollar check. After the cameras were off, I got to meet with the maker of the game, and we played a couple of games. I couldn't beat him even once, and I was glad that I wasn't facing him for the money.

His assistants ushered me to a stack of papers; wherever they told me to sign, I did.

I celebrated by drinking sparkling apple cider in a champagne glass with my father as we relaxed in the Jacuzzi.

"Dad, now that I have won this money, can you come home so we can be a family again?"

My father had tears in his eyes and said, "Yes, son. Yes. I want us to be a family again."

My family met us at the airport, and I was pleasantly surprised to see Roxanne.

I had never seen my mother run so quickly as when she spotted my father; there were no visible signs of an arthritic knee. Alicia came up to me and gave me a big hug, which I wasn't expecting. Roxanne was next and gave me a long hug and a kiss.

"I want to ask you something."

"What?" I answered calmly.

"I want to be your girl."

I had heard these words millions of times in my head and answered in my most assured voice, "No doubt. No doubt."

My siblings were getting acquainted with Dad, someone they didn't know, and I spent most of the time with Roxanne, sitting on my lap as I stared into her pretty brown eyes.

This was a picture perfect moment, and I didn't want the day to end.

It was a pleasure to be in school. The way everyone treated me, I knew that they had seen me on TV. Even Max was a groupie. He actually got my lunch and acted like my bodyguard as students came up to my table to speak to me.

Me and Roxanne sat like the King and Queen, while all the peasants wanted to get a look at royalty. Peter was also sitting at our table and even let Michael soak in the glory.

Michael said, "Wow, Justin. The probability of you winning was very slim. Very slim. I calculated the odds on my computer last night. You had a better chance of getting hit by lightning three times in a row."

"Well, Michael. I guess that probability thing didn't affect me. I am special, and I knew I was going to be rich some day. I knew it would happen."

I made my way to math class, and the first person I wanted to see was Mr. Jones.

I had practiced a hundred times last night on how I would diss him. When I entered the classroom, I spoke in my most sarcastic tone, "I'll *probably* buy a home today. Or *probably* buy a car, or better yet I *probably* should buy you a new toupee. The one you have on *probably* won't last you much longer."

The class burst into laughter.

I wasn't finished with him yet; he wasn't going to get away that easily.

"I guess the odds are in my favor. Did I not tell you that I was going to be rich? Don't look surprised. I could *probably* buy your measly salary. Maybe I'll hire you to wash my clothes or clean my house or car, or maybe you can be my butler."

Mr. Jones slammed a math textbook down on his desk and told me to go to the Principal's office.

I made myself comfortable in Principal Frank's office. And even yawned as he told me that he was tired of my antics, and, if I didn't watch myself, I wouldn't graduate on time.

"Graduate?" I yelled back. "I'm rich. I don't need to graduate anymore. I just skipped several years of tests, teachers, and school. Not to mention that crummy lunch you pass off as food."

Principal Frank shook his head and said, "You still need an education. Something to fall back on."

"The only thing I need to fall back on is a sofa or a bed," I answered with a smile. "Let me put you up on a little secret. Today will be my last day. School is for people looking to get money, and now I have it. Maybe I'll invite you to my house one day."

It felt good saying that. When I exited his office, I went straight home.

My father was on the couch watching TV, and he asked me what I was doing home. I ignored his question, went to my room, and went straight to sleep.

I woke up when my mother and father came into my room. Even though my mother had her back to me, she nodded in agreement as my father spoke. "Principal Frank called and told us that you have decided to quit school. We have decided that it is your life, and you can make any decisions you want. We respect your decisions. If you don't want to go to school, you don't have to."

I blinked a couple of times to make sure I wasn't dreaming, but it was as real as it could be. My mother left the room silently, and my father sat with me.

"We also agreed that the money is yours, and you can spend it on anything you like. I will come with you tomorrow and co-sign on a bank account, being you're underage and all, and we will all follow your lead."

As I laid my head down on the pillow, I figured it was going to be a long day.

I was looking forward to going house shopping, clothes shopping, car shopping, furniture shopping, and any other kind of shopping I could think of.

I wanted this neighborhood to be a distant memory. I didn't really like people looking at me in my building. I once heard of a lottery winner who decided to live in his same neighborhood after he won his money. They kidnapped his wife and kids, and he had to pay to get them back.

I did not want to be shaken down.

It felt good as the bank manager jumped through hoops when he realized I was opening an account. Money sure gets people to move quickly. He even got me an ATM card right away, and I was able to get any loan I wanted from the bank. Those things usually took five to fifteen business days and loads of background checks. But he had it sent from the home office in Las Vegas. *Now that's service.* I didn't even wait for the check to clear. I had full access to my money.

I left the bank with an ATM card, credit card, checks, and a couple of phone numbers, which I threw away. The girls were cute, but I only had eyes for Roxanne.

Next was the car dealership.

As soon as I entered, I saw the car of my dreams. It was the Bentley Continental GTC convertible. One word described it. Sweet.

We were in the dealership for about twenty-five minutes, but no one came over to us. I went over to a sales associate and asked him for a specific breakdown of the car.

"That is $200,000."

I hated being brushed off. "I didn't ask you the price. I want to know the features."

After a couple more brief words and my voice escalating, the dealership manager came over to us.

"Is there a problem, gentlemen?"

My father responded, "Your employee was rude and didn't treat us like customers. Just because we don't look all distinguished and all doesn't mean we can't afford it."

"Sorry, gentlemen. Please come into my office, and I'll answer all your questions."

He gave us a detailed breakdown of the car. After telling us about all the extra features, I told him we'd take four of them: different models and different features.

The manager had that paperwork right in front of me quicker than I could blink, but I said I would not sign anything unless the sales associate apologized.

I heard the manager telling him my request. After a quick back and forth, he came over and apologized. I knew it was embarrassing, but I didn't care.

As I exited, I said, "Never judge a book by its cover. Anyone who comes through that door could be a potential customer and should be treated accordingly."

We drove one of the cars off the showroom floor, and I rode shotgun as we dipped in and out of traffic in the city.

All eyes were on us, and I felt like a celebrity.

We opened up the engine on the highway, and I told my father to drive through our old neighborhood just for kicks.

Things were pretty much the same, and I was surprised when I noticed a "for sale" sign at the house we used to live in.

We went in, and I realized how different the house was.

A lot of renovation had taken place, and the house was even bigger than it was before.

The owner, who said he was relocating to Florida, told us the asking price was $1.5 million. After my father explained that we would write him a check right then and there, he sold it to us for $1 million. For an extra $100,000, the owner said he would even move out by nighttime.

My father answered, "We have a deal."

Usually it could take people months before they could move into their purchased house. That was one of the perks with having money. They say money talks. Well, today it was speaking like a megaphone. With money, the impossible seemed to be possible.

We made our way back to the city, where we went to a classy furniture store in Manhattan and had my father pick out the furniture that resembled what my mother had five years ago.

Later on that night, we took everyone back up to Selden, New York, and my mother broke down in tears when I handed her the keys for the house. Mama kept repeating that it didn't matter where we lived and how much money we had. But I knew she was happy. We were all finally back together. Back to the good life where we belonged.

Mama couldn't control herself the next morning when they showed up with her brand new car. She almost fainted because she said that she had never seen something that red before. It was custom painted candy apple red, and I had vanity plates that read, "F A I T H."

Mama hugged me so hard that I could barely breathe. Even though I pleaded with her, she said, "Work never killed no one. Last time I was in this house, I didn't work. This time, I don't care what is going on. I will be working."

After some convincing from my father, my mother quit her first job, but she still worked as a waitress at the restaurant. Many people thought she owned the restaurant when they saw what she pulled up in.

It was the weekend, and I had a stretch limo pick up me, Alicia, and Marcus and take us back to my old neighborhood.

As we got to my old neighborhood, I saw Fred hanging out by the bus stop, and he looked suspiciously as the limo slowly rolled up to him.

I brought the window down and when Fred saw it was me, he was surprised. "Justin, my man. I heard you big time now. Good to see you. You are really doing it big."

"What's up with you?"

"You know. Trying to make it do what it do."

"Hop in, and let's go shopping."

"Alright, bet. Let's go."

As Fred got in, Alicia gave me a funny look because she hated Fred. When he said hello to her, she just rolled her eyes and looked in the other direction.

I picked up Peter and Roxanne next, and we went to Jamaica Avenue in Queens. I bought sneakers, shoes, watches, hats, belts, video games, jackets, shirts, and t-shirts. I didn't bother looking at any price tags, I just handed over my credit card. I bought Fred, Peter, and Roxanne anything they wanted as well, and we had about 75 bags to carry as we left the store.

Alicia and Marcus weren't into the clothes thing, and I bought them every reading material imaginable.

I even bought books for Albert, along with everything that had Teenage Mutant Ninja Turtles on it.

Afterwards, we went to eat in downtown Brooklyn. We paid $5000 to close the whole restaurant off to the public for two hours. We were eating, drinking, and laughing, while people outside were looking through the window trying to see who was in there.

I saw a couple of flashes as people were taking pictures like the paparazzi; I guess they had seen me on TV.

I was feeling generous and ordered some hors d'oeuvres to be given to people who were standing near the window.

I didn't even look at the bill as they handed it to me. I just gave the receipt to Marcus, who put it in his bookbag with the rest.

It wasn't until we had finished shopping and Marcus, who was adding up all the receipts on his calculator, told me that I had spent $50,000. But it was nothing to a boss, I thought. I had money to burn. I was three million dollars richer.

I had to have a cell phone, so I got the latest one that was on the market, which ran me $600. I bought one for everyone, except for Albert who didn't know how to operate one. I told everyone not to worry about the bill because it was under my name and I would take care of everything.

It was a tiring day. After dropping off Fred, Roxanne, and Peter, I went up to Mr. Saks' apartment and knocked on the door. After he flushed the toilet then went back and used it again, he finally came to the door.

"Here's the big celebrity."

"Hey, Mr. Saks."

"I noticed your family has moved out."

"Yeah, we are onto bigger and better things."

"I see. How are you adjusting to your new school?"

"I dropped out, but my siblings are adjusting just fine."

I saw a speech ready to come out, and I was relieved when my cell phone rang. "Got to go, Mr. Saks. I'll see you around."

As I came downstairs, I saw Fred still standing outside the building, and I told him that I would have a limo pick him up in the morning and bring him to my crib.

Everyone was out of the house early, and Fred arrived at 10:30.

His eyes were on the ground as he saw where I lived, and he was speechless when he saw the size of my house.

"Who would of thunk it? Playing those fantasy video games can let you cake off like this. Maybe I should get me a VGA2 and practice," Fred said, looking at our swimming pool. "Nah. I love the streets, it's intriguing to me. Actually, it is like a video game, and I've been winning for four years. I haven't been beaten yet."

I smiled and said, "I owe it all to you."

"It's nothing. I guess I don't need to show you how I get my money after all, huh."

"I guess not."

I had to fix Fred lunch because my mother had insisted that we didn't have a maid this time. As we watched TV on my sixty-five-inch plasma screen TV, I heard the bell ring.

A burly man who looked like he was in his early twenties told me I had a delivery. After signing the papers, I told Fred I had a surprise for him.

Fred came outside, and I threw him a set of car keys. He couldn't control himself. Fred had me in a tight bear hug and began rocking me back and forth when he saw the chocolate brown hardtop convertible limited edition Bentley with chrome and brown rims to match, eggshell interior, navigation, and all the other trimmings that could go inside a car.

I made sure that he had personalized vanity plates saying "F R E D."

"Word. This is for me? This is hard body. You hear me? Hard body."

Right beside Fred's car was my new car, which was custom painted powder blue. I bought a sedan because I didn't want to move my seat when someone had to get in the back seats.

I didn't even have my license yet, but I was turning fifteen soon. It wouldn't be long before I reached eighteen; then I could drive all by myself.

My life was a dream come true, and I felt like a man.

I paid the lights, gas, water, heat, cell phones, cable, insurance on all four cars, landscaping, pool maintenance—everything in the house.

I didn't have to write too many checks because I decided to have all the companies withdraw the money from my account. That way I would never have any late payments. I learned that from my parents' inability to pay bills on time.

I gave Roxanne $30,000 to help her mother retain a lawyer after she got busted for shoplifting in the mall. That was a waste of money because she had been in trouble with the law before and had to serve a year in jail.

Roxanne was pretty upset, and I spent another $10,000 on a shopping spree to cheer her up.

I also gave Max $10,000 because he said that he had this business he was trying to start on the Internet.

Fred picked me up at 10:00 every morning. We would drive around, shop, and blow money on all kind of things.

After I got back home I would sit on the couch with my eyes glued to the television with the telephone in my hand.

I ordered all kinds of things and store them in the basement. The UPS man was so familiar with me that he would call me up beforehand to tell me he was coming.

I was quickly becoming Aunt Clara.

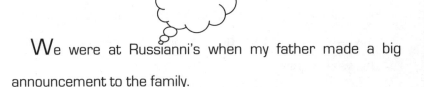

We were at Russianni's when my father made a big announcement to the family.

"I have great news. I got a new job in Manhattan."

Everyone was happy, especially Mama, who had my father in a bear hug rocking him back and forth.

"That's great dad, what will you be doing?" I asked.

"I'll be starting in the mailroom again but don't you worry. As sure as my name is Phillip Stanford I'll work my tail off and maybe I'll get to the top again."

Things couldn't be better and we enjoyed dinner and my mother even went up to sing *We are Family* by *Sister Sledge* during karaoke time.

Six months later

I was playing video games in my room when Marcus called me. "You have a letter from the IRS."

"Let me see it. Bring it here."

The letter informed me that I hadn't filed a tax return, and I looked at the date—November 21, 2006—and scrunched it up in a ball and threw it in the garbage.

I called Fred because I didn't want to ask my parents; plus, if anyone knew what was up, he would have the right answers.

"Yo, you don't have to file any taxes. You only file taxes if you are older, man. Like an adult. You are still a baby. Plus people only pay taxes if they have a job. You didn't work anywhere this year, right?"

"Of course not," I responded. "I haven't worked a day in my life."

I hung up the phone and felt relieved.

It was January, and boy was it cold.

I was on my way out when I heard the phone ring.

I answered it on the third ring and a man began speaking,

"Hello, can I speak to Justin Stanford? This is Mr. Birchman calling."

I hated those annoying telemarketers. They called non-stop.

"I am not interested in buying anything," I answered, annoyed.

The voice on the phone got more assertive. "I am not selling anything. I have an urgent matter that needs to be taken care of immediately. If you are Justin Stanford, I will tell you what this call is in regards to. Otherwise, I will call back to speak to him."

I no longer wanted to play cat and mouse and confidently said, "I am Justin Stanford. How can I help you?"

"I am calling to inform you that you have not filed a tax return for the current year, and our records indicate that—"

"Look here. Mr. Birchman. I just turned fifteen and haven't worked a day in my life. You've gotten me mixed up with someone else. My name is common. Get a life and go chase someone else. I don't have time for this."

"Well, Mr. Stanford. I assure you that I do have the right person."

I said in a calm voice, "Oh yes, I am so sorry. I think someone from your office named Tone called me last week. "

"Excuse me. Tone who?"

"Dial Tone."

I slammed the phone down as hard as I could.

He obviously wasn't listening to a word I was saying.

I left the house, and Fred and I laughed when I told him what happened.

"You crazy. I bet he won't call back again."

"Well, if he does, he will be speaking to Mr. Dial Tone again."

A year later

It was a hot summer day, and I sat on an uncomfortable wooden chair, listening as the master of ceremonies spoke at the podium.

"Congratulations, graduates of Selden Junior High School."

Marcus had graduated with honors and was on his way to a prep school out of state on full academic scholarship.

My parents were happy, and Alicia vowed she would be doing the same in about five years. Albert agreed. "I am going to be the smartest boy in my school, too."

I supported Marcus by clapping as loudly as I could.

I wanted to somehow drown out the concept of school in my mind forever. I had been out of school almost two years and started thinking about George working in that electronic store for minimum wage.

Better him than me, I thought.

The ceremony seemed extremely long and drawn out; by the time Marcus came up to speak—being the Valedictorian and all—I was fast asleep.

My mother had to shame me into staying awake by kicking me with her high heels. That hurt.

I heard Marcus end his speech by saying, "Material things will come and go. The only thing you get to keep forever is what you know. So keep educating yourself and you'll be rich beyond belief."

The crowd gave my brother a standing ovation. Even though my leg was killing me, I got up as well.

I thought his words were kind of corny, but I guess that was what people wanted to hear.

I looked at my phone and saw that Max had left me a voicemail message.

I listened as Max told me business was booming, and that, since I gave him the start up money, he wanted to throw a party for me in Manhattan.

Max customized t-shirts that had been selling for $150 apiece. It was amazing how they were selling like hotcakes, but I had to admit they were fly. I had even seen some rappers wearing them in their videos.

I got in touch with Max after calling him a couple of times unsuccessfully. I told him not to go through all that trouble and just have it at my house, but would have to provide the food, entertainment, drinks, and music.

° ○ ○

It was a cool and sunny Saturday afternoon when the festivities began.

There were about 350 people at my house, and most of them were Max's customers.

Max was the life of the party and mingled with everyone.

He had transformed from super thug to a young, professional, polite, and charming entrepreneur.

"Max, you are really doing it big. Why are you still going to school?"

"To get an education. Why else? I have to at least go to graduate school."

"What for? You already have money."

"So what? I still want to educate myself. Money comes and goes, but knowledge reigns supreme. I have to have something to fall back on. Education is the best crutch made. It fits all genders, sizes, shapes, ethnicities and races.

The more informed I am, the more someone won't be able to take advantage of me," Max said, as he inhaled a hotdog with beans on it.

"Okay, Pastor Max. I didn't know you could preach so well."

"Funny, Just. I am a changed person. School didn't mean nothing to me before. But I have seen the light, Hallelujah, Hallelujah," he said, trying to sound like one of those TV evangelists.

Max went to give me a pound but instead handed me a check for $10,000.

"Seriously, Justin. Good looking on the money. You were the only one that ever believed in me."

"It is nothing to a boss."

This was the first time I had been back to the bank since I had opened my account. I had to ask the teller if I had filled out the deposit slip correctly. She had to destroy the one I handed her and helped me correctly fill out the second one.

After she took the check, she said, "Hold on a minute. I have to speak with the manager."

"For what? Do you want to see some ID?"

"No sir. It should only take a minute."

I waited for thirty minutes, and I was wondering if she had taken a lunch break or something.

She finally came back and began talking to me but didn't look me in the eye.

"I have to inform you that a hold has been placed on your account."

"There must be a mistake. Check again."

"I am sorry, Mr. Stanford. I can't discuss this with you any further. You have to talk to the manager."

I waited another hour to speak to the manager.

He shuffled papers on his desk and didn't even look at me as he spoke in a monotone voice. "I see. I see."

"What do you see?" I answered in an annoyed and loud voice.

That caught his attention. "Please sir. Keep your voice down. This is a place of business. If you continue in this manner, I will have to ask you to leave."

When he motioned to the security guard to come closer, I told him that would not be necessary.

"The IRS has put a hold on your account and a levy on your home and anything else you may own."

He continued shuffling through his papers. "I am not able to give you specifics, but what I will say is that they claim you have not filed taxes in the year 2006, for starters."

"But I didn't work that year. I was fourteen years old."

"Well, I don't know. I am not the IRS. I am a bank manager. If you want any information, you are to contact them. The check you tried to deposit will be sent straight to the IRS for owed taxes. Have a good day."

I wanted to take his stapler off his desk, staple his mouth shut, and then maybe his eyeballs, but I kept my cool because the security guard looked is if he would have knocked me into next week.

I went straight home, ran upstairs to my closet, and looked through every piece of mail that I hadn't open.

In the past two years, I had a total of twenty-five letters addressed to me that had the sender name of the IRS.

I opened the most recent one first and saw that they were trying to contact me and if I wanted to set up a payment plan, they would be willing to assist me.

I grabbed the phone and called them.

My luck was at an all-time low because, when I got through, I heard the voice of Mr. Birchman.

"It is good to finally hear from you. Last time we spoke, you introduced me to Mr. Dial Tone. I bet you thought that was pretty funny. Anyway, how can I help you today?"

"I still don't understand why I need to pay taxes. I told you that I was a minor and fourteen. Actually, I am sixteen now. I have never worked a day in my life."

"You are right. You have never worked a day in your life."

I felt relieved. We were finally getting somewhere.

"Do you remember that check that you received for three million dollars?"

"Yes. What does that have to do with anything?"

"Well, don't you think you have to pay taxes on that?"

"It wasn't something I worked for. I won it in a contest."

"Did you sign any papers when you received that money?"

"Yes, I did."

"Well, obviously you weren't aware of the section that stated that the winner is responsible for all taxes on the winnings. It's the law. We tried to explain to you, but you wouldn't give us a chance. My calculations show that you owe

$1,076,375 for the federal tax. State and local taxes are $330,645."

I felt empty inside. I didn't know what to do. I had to think fast.

"Well, I could sell some of my things. I have loads of stuff in my basement. Then, if necessary, I will set up a payment plan."

"It is too late for that. Our experience has shown people will say they will give us the money. Then they sell all their things and skip town. I wouldn't want you running off to Mexico or somewhere else. We are not willing to take that chance. We will be auctioning off everything that has your name attached to it, big ticket items like your home, etc. in two months."

That last comment felt like a splinter in my eye. What was I going to tell my family? Where would we live?

It was hard to get the words out at dinnertime, but I had never seen my family so quiet. Alicia just looked up at the ceiling as I talked.

I told them I didn't have any money to pay the utilities and asked did anyone have any suggestions on how we were going to pay the bills.

Marcus took out his calculator.

"Well, Mama and Dad would have to work twenty-four hours a day, seven days a week, to pay all the utilities alone, and that is with a fifteen-dollar raise. Car insurance and other amenities aren't even included. We wouldn't be able to pay those things."

No one finished dinner that night.

I woke up earlier than I ever have since I had won the money and got on the train with my father as he traveled to work.

He had gotten quite popular at his job and they allowed me to follow him around as he delivered mail to the employees.

My father took me out to this burger joint for lunch.

"Dad, I am so sorry. I thought I had things under control. How could I be so stupid? Spend all that money and not know what was going on?"

My father looked genuinely concerned and rubbed my head. "Son, I know the feeling. There are so many things you don't know about me. The reason why I had to move to Japan was that I was stealing money from the company I worked for. We were living so lavishly, and I wanted to impress everyone. That is why I threw all those parties and stuff. That is when I started hanging out with people that did drugs and alcohol and couldn't stop indulging in both.

The President of the company wanted to send me to jail. I had cost them millions. But I pleaded and told them I was willing to work it off. My lawyer worked out all the details, and that is why I had to move to Japan. I had to start from the ground up and build the company in Japan, training very inexperienced salesmen to reach very high, even almost, impossible quotas each month. I didn't receive a paycheck for five years. They provided me with only food and shelter. That was why I always needed money."

I felt so stupid. Thinking my father was a leech and didn't care about us.

"I was lucky. I was able to repay my debt by working it off right before I met up with you in Jamaica. I was so out of control, son. I had nothing to fall back on. No education. Nothing. I never prepared for the future because I had done better than most of my friends. I felt good telling them that I was making more money than them and how stupid they were to be wasting time in school.

All of those same friends are doing better than me now. Because school gave them the security of being able to have several options and be able to always start at a certain level."

I listened intently. This was the most I had ever heard my father speak, and I didn't want to miss a word.

"I can't be part of certain opportunities because I don't even have a high school diploma. These days, you need a graduate degree just to be competitive. Check it out. I always have to start at the bottom and—guess what?—I am old now. I may never make it back to the top, but I want better for you.

No one can take away your education. No one. That is the one thing that remains with you after you have received it."

I felt like such a dumpkoff and wondered why I never thought about these things before.

"Did you and Mama know I was going to blow the money?"

"Yes, we did. That is why we gave you total control of everything. We felt that was the only way that you would hopefully learn your lesson.

Your mother and I love you dearly, and money will come and go. We know that. But knowledge is forever; hopefully you will learn a lesson from this that you may never forget. They say sometimes you have to experience things for yourself before you get the picture. Money isn't everything, and with money comes responsibility. You have to be knowledgeable or smart or educated to handle it. That is why education is important."

It was seven o'clock in the morning when I got out of bed.

Mr. Saks used the bathroom several times during the night. The plumbing was much better; when Mr. Saks went, I didn't have to worry about me or my bed getting wet.

I went to the bathroom, jumped in the shower, and got ready for my first day back to school.

It was me, Albert, and Alicia walking to school that morning.

Math was my first class, and I was happy that I had stayed up late last night getting in some practice problems.

I answered every question correctly that Mr. Jones had on the board.

I felt an A coming up this marking period. Which would be a 360-degree turn. I received A's before, but they usually stood for ABSENT.

It was kind of embarrassing being sixteen years old in the eighth grade, but I was going to work my tail off and go to summer school. Then maybe I could get out of high school before I turned twenty.

As I sat in class, I thought of my friends. I missed everyone.

I hadn't seen Fred much at all. He wrecked the car I gave him trying to run away from some people he owed money. He has been on the run after jumping bail when he got caught with a gun. When they catch him, he'll be serving a mandatory three-and-a-half year sentence in jail.

Peter was entering his third year of high school, and Max actually graduated early. Roxanne moved to the Bronx with her mother and is a straight 'A' student, getting a full scholarship to college.

Roxanne told me that she didn't want to date anymore; she didn't need any distractions.

School had a whole new meaning for me. I was learning so much that before I knew, it was lunchtime.

It was so funny, but as I sat in the lunchroom all by myself, I thought of Michael.

I told myself I wasn't going to be a statistic.

A couple of kids snickered as they looked at my outfit.

My style was so two years ago. Even though I had a lot of outfits, they were outdated.

I didn't care about those things anymore. I had much bigger fish to fry. I was trying to get my *education on*.

When I got home, I saw a letter addressed to me from Marcus. I got a new letter from him every week, and Marcus had convinced me to be part of the RAUTAM [Reading Allows You To Achieve More] club. They are a tough group. I've been reading a book a week, and reading has definitely changed my outlook on life.

I have new information from many different sources. Marcus kids me every now and again, telling me that I should have read the contract I signed and been much smarter with my money.

Marcus was right. It's better to make an informed decision instead of taking someone else's word for it.

I looked through my mail and saw letters from the IRS. This time I made sure to open them immediately.

They informed me that my old house only sold for $500,000, which was lower than I paid for it.

I read somewhere that house prices always went lower when they were sold on rainy days, and they auctioned off my other possessions (cars, etcetera) and got another $400,000.

I can't even think of getting anything on credit.

I still owe Uncle Sam about another $400,000. There is no way out until it is paid. No exceptions. IRS debt is forever.

At 6:00 p.m., I ate dinner with my family. I looked at Mama, Dad, Albert, and Alicia, and even our small apartment and felt content.

Content has been Alicia's favorite new word, and I didn't even have to ask her the meaning. I was a reading juggernaut, and I had my pocket dictionary handy at all times.

After dessert, which was peach cobbler, I told my parents I was going to see Mr. Saks.

Mr. Saks was happy to see me at his door.

"How you doing, young man?" Mr. Saks said as he stood in the doorway.

"Good, Mr. Saks. I just wanted to borrow a new book."

Mr. Saks hurriedly found something new to give me and said, "Your mother told me how focused you are in school now. Congratulations."

I cracked a smile. "You know, what can I say? Got to have them A's."

Mr. Saks chuckled and said he would see me again next week to discuss the book.

I went back to my apartment and watched as my father danced with my mother. This was weird, because there wasn't any music playing.

"Hey, son. I just got a phone call from my boss saying I got a promotion. One step at a time, son. One step at a time."

My mother was happy and told my father we would celebrate this weekend when Marcus came home.

My mother went back to her room and told us she was going to do some research for her paper.

I was so proud of her. She was back to school part time. This was her second semester in college.

Before I retired for bed, I read a quote Mr. Saks had taped to the inside of the book. *Learn while you are young, and not while you're old, that getting a good education is better than gold, for silver and gold will melt away, but a good education will never decay.*

I closed the book and looked over to my left. Alicia was cuddled up under the sheets, and I heard Albert snoring like an old man below me on the bottom bunk.

I turned back over and began thinking of the house in Selden, the cars, clothes, limos, parties, and the life I had.

But this life was okay for now. Money didn't solve my problems; it came with a lot of responsibility.

I'll be more responsible when I graduate college—maybe a PhD before it is all said and done—and run my own company.

Whoever said money is everything is a liar. I am rich beyond imagination.